Pauline Cl

PAULINE CLARKE was born in Nottinghamshire, England, in 1921, and studied English literature at Somerville College, Oxford. She has written plays, stories, and articles, for adults as well as for children, and has published several books under the name Helen Clare.

Clarke's inspiration for the story of the Twelves was the band of wooden soldiers given to Branwell Brontë more than a hundred fifty years ago, when he was eight, the same age as Max. Branwell was the brother of three famous British writers: Charlotte, who wrote *Jane Eyre*; Emily, who wrote *Wuthering Heights*; and Anne, who wrote *Agnes Grey*. The Twelves served as some of the characters in the four children's first attempts at writing.

Pauline Clarke said that "I was fascinated by the Twelves' names and ages, which Branwell listed in his story 'The History of the Young Men.' I noted down 'Butter Crashey, Captain, 140,' and the rest, and in due course I saw how I wanted to use them. My aim was to keep, but develop, the soldiers' characters as Branwell had outlined them."

The Return of The Twelves, which was first published in 1962, received the 1963 Carnegie Medal in England, the German Jugend Buchpreis, a Lewis Carroll Shelf Award, and was selected for the Hans Christian Andersen Honor List in 1964.

In 1969, Pauline Clarke married Peter Hunter Blair, a professor at Cambridge University. She lives with her family near Cambridge, England.

YEARLING CLASSICS

Works of lasting literary merit by English
and American classic and contemporary writers

HANS BRINKER, OR THE SILVER SKATES, Mary Mapes Dodge
EIGHT COUSINS, OR THE AUNT HILL, Louisa May Alcott
FIVE LITTLE PEPPERS AND HOW THEY GREW, Margaret Sidney
THE MIDNIGHT FOLK, John Masefield
FIVE CHILDREN AND IT, E. Nesbit
THE PRINCE AND THE PAUPER, Mark Twain
THE PRINCESS AND THE GOBLIN, George MacDonald
ROSE IN BLOOM, Louisa May Alcott
TOM'S MIDNIGHT GARDEN, Philippa Pearce
LITTLE LORD FAUNTLEROY, Frances Hodgson Burnett
THE BOOK OF DRAGONS, E. Nesbit
REBECCA OF SUNNYBROOK FARM, Kate Douglas Wiggin
A GIRL OF THE LIMBERLOST, Gene Stratton Porter
DOCTOR DOLITTLE: A TREASURY, Hugh Lofting
FOUR DOLLS, Rumer Godden

YEARLING BOOKS are designed especially to entertain and
enlighten young people. Charles F. Reasoner, Professor
Emeritus of Children's Literature and Reading, New York
University, is consultant to this series.

For a complete listing of all Yearling titles, write to
Dell Publishing Co., Inc., Promotion Department,
P.O. Box 3000, Pine Brook, N.J. 07058.

The Return
of the Twelves

Pauline Clarke

Illustrated by Cecil Leslie

Afterword by Katherine Paterson

Published by
Dell Publishing Co., Inc.
1 Dag Hammarskjold Plaza
New York, NY 10017

This work was first published in Great Britain by The Bodley Head under the title *The Twelve and the Genii*, and in the U.S.A. by Coward-McCann Inc., a division of the Putnam Publishing Group Inc., under the title *The Return of the Twelves*.

Yearling® TM 913705, Dell Publishing Co., Inc.

ISBN: 0-440-47536-8

RL: 7.1

Printed in the United States of America

November 1986

10 9 8 7 6 5 4 3 2 1

W

May the Four Genii forgive
us for playing with their soldiers

Contents

Chapter 1

The Attic

Max sat on the bare stairs below the attic, wondering whether to tell anyone.

His socks were round his ankles. It had suddenly become too hot for socks but it had not yet dawned upon Max to take them off. His hands drummed tunes on the step beside him, or played the harp down the wooden banisters. At short intervals, he put finger and thumb into his mouth, picked out his huge round gob-stopper sweet, observed what colour it now was, and put it back. All the time he was frowning slightly, and when he was not making a noise with his hands, he listened. His rather large ears stuck out from his head as if they were the larger for listening.

There it was again.

He stopped his loud sucking, and gulped, in order to listen. His eyes were wide open, his eyebrows high up, and one cheek was swollen into a great bulge with the sweet. He looked like a deformed, surprised dwarf.

Of course they would say it was rats.

Anyone would.

Or birds under the roof.

Pit pat tipper tapper scrabble stamp. Whee. Whish. Sizzle whizzle. That was the whispering.

He supposed that, to them, that size, it was proper speaking. If you were that size, and said something, that is what it would sound like. Even if you shouted like old Buster, the sergeant at school who gave them P.T., it would not sound loud. Max imagined, with great pleasure, old Buster shrinking to their size. How he would roar with terror. He would think he was going to vanish, and every-

The Attic

one would laugh. And his roar would gradually get quieter and whinier as he shrank.

Tip tap tip tap tip tap tip tap stamp.

Now this time it was so regular that only silly people would think it was rats. They might think it was a thrush breaking a snail shell; or a woodpecker at a tree's bark. Max knew it was none of these things.

He knew quite well what it was and in a minute he would get up, if he could without making a creak, and look at them. Meanwhile, should he fetch Jane, perhaps, while it was going on, and tell only her? Just Jane.

She would have to believe it if she saw it.

But if she made a noise, then they might freeze, they *would*, and she would laugh at him and call him batty.

His heart felt big with such a thrilling secret inside it.

He did not know how *not* to tell someone.

But of course, once he had told, then it was no longer his secret. There would be the joy of telling, of showing Jane, of proving it, and then there would be Jane wanting to join in everything and enjoy it too. Also, it might be better to wait till they were not frightened of him. They still were, they would still freeze if he went in. He was longing to be real friends with them, he could think of the funniest things they could do, if they would only let him pick them up, and trust him. Perhaps it would be better to get them to trust him first, before he even told Jane.

As stealthy as an animal he stood, turned, knelt by the attic door, and put his twinkling grey eye to the keyhole.

There they were. Three rows of four. Drilling.

It was funny to see them drilling so smartly with their uniform so shabby. There was hardly any paint left at all. It must have been scarlet once. Perhaps if they trusted him, they would let him paint them. Give them a coat of paint. Max grinned. This was exactly right.

Jane came to the landing below and she saw Max kneeling at the attic door. He turned his head, with one eye still screwed up and the other cheek as fat as a golf ball. Jane shrieked with laughter.

"Max, what are you doing, you look absolutely cracked," she

said. "I didn't know this was where you said your prayers."

"Oh, shut *up*," hissed Max, through one side of his mouth.

"What is it? One of your secret games? I know: you're just going to be beheaded! Who are you? Sir Walter Raleigh?"

Max stood up, pulled a face as best he could though hindered by his sweet, and remained silent.

"You can choke on those things, you know. We're all going to Bradford. You've got to come."

"Who says? Dirty old Bradford," said Max; though Jane could not understand him.

"We've got to buy things. For the house. And Mummy says she's sick of getting rooms straight and needs to spend some money; I don't blame her, do you?"

They had only been here a week, in this old farm-house. They were all so glad to be out of a town that they could not stop saying so.

"I'm going to stay here," Max said; this is what he said, but Jane had to guess.

"What? Do take that sweet out."

"Maxy!" called Mrs. Morley. "Come on, quickly."

Max went to the next landing, leaned over the banisters, took out his sweet and said:

"Mummy, can I please stay here, I have something entirely special I want to do."

When Max, who was eight, made speeches with long words, his mother could not deny him. He had learned this and used it when he needed to.

"You'll be sorry, you know. We'll be gone two or three hours. All of us. Daddy as well," she said.

"I shan't be sorry, I'll be glad," he answered.

"What about tea?"

"Aren't you even coming back to tea?"

"We *may* not. You can have a piece of cake and two buns. And bread if you want it. Mind the bread knife."

"Yes," he said.

"Good-bye, darling. Bill's around in the farmyard if you want him. Don't do stupid things, will you?"

"No," said Max. "I never do."

Jane jeered. So did Philip, who had joined them.

"Isn't he coming, our little man?" said Philip.

Max put his stained orange tongue out at Philip, stuck in his sweet again and turned his back on them.

"What is he up to, Jane?"

"I don't know," she said. "When I came up, he was either saying his prayers, or being beheaded, outside the attic. I don't know which. Kneeling down."

"Both, I expect. Naturally," Philip said, "you'd say your prayers if you were about to depart this life."

"He makes up so many things in his mind," said Mrs. Morley, "it may be anything."

Chapter 2

The Patriarch

Max waited until he heard the motor-car doors slam, and the engine purr and sing. Then he did, in fact, race down to his own room, and lean out of the window, in time to see the number-plate of the Land Rover disappear out of the yard. For a minute he felt sorry and lonely.

Then he went quietly up the attic stairs again, and looked through the keyhole.

The wooden soldiers stood exactly as he had seen them when Jane interrupted. They had not moved a tenth of an inch. They were as dead as ninepins. They had frozen again. Max sighed, enraged. This would be a sell, if he had prevented himself going with the others for nothing.

All the same, he did not give up hope. He had seen them move twice now, and what you saw you believed. (Max also believed many things he did not see, like everyone else.) The gob-stopper was becoming more manageable now, and as he knelt there, Max turned it over and over in his mouth. Suddenly, he crunched it all up with determination and impatience. He decided to go in.

He wandered round the attic, pretending to be busy looking at things, but all the while keeping half a cautious eye upon them. It felt to him as if they were keeping cautious eyes on him. It was like two cats, casually looking away from each other, but really each wondering if the other were going to pounce.

It seemed much more than a week that they had been here. It had seemed a lovely house to come to, and as if it were theirs at once and always had been. He remembered the time they first came up here, to the attic, carrying the stool, the boat and the drum.

The Patriarch

Mrs. Morley had said: "Now, we won't banish Great-grandpa's Ashanti things for ever, but as I don't know quite where they're going, will you take them carefully up to the attic, please."

Philip, Jane and Max were only too eager to explore the attic. Philip had seized the heavy, carved, wooden stool with its curved seat, Jane had clasped the curious-shaped skin-covered oblong drum to her chest, and Max had taken the carved model canoe. Their great-grandfather had been a missionary on the Gold Coast of West Africa. He had gone up the Niger further than any other missionary before him, no doubt in just such a boat, he had talked to kings who thought it was quite all right to kill people for sacrifices, he had seen the pits where they threw them and huts that were full of skulls.

Max now came to the stool, sat down upon its curve which fitted the sitter so comfortably, and looked squarely at the soldiers. On just such a stool, their mother had often told them, were crowned the kings of Ashanti. She had been told by Grandma, who was the daughter of the missionary.

Max had stayed behind that first time, to explore thoroughly. He had stamped round the attic, just as he had seen the surveyor do, jumping on boards and tapping walls. He had been rewarded by finding the loose board near the window. Max never left things half explored. He got his knife, levered up the board, and found the dirty, torn roll of rag in which were the old soldiers. Twelve of them.

"After all," said Max aloud, "I did rescue you from a living death."

He thought this was a fine expression, he had read it in some book lately. Although they were so old and knocked about, it was exciting and mysterious to find them hidden, and to wonder who had hidden them. Added to this, when he brought them to show the family his mother had said:

"Max! How interesting. Do take care of them, because I should think they're really old, they ought to be in a museum."

"How old, Mummy? How old, Daddy?" Max said, clutching them in his two hands.

"Careful, they look a bit frail," his father had said. And he took

one, and scrutinized it. "Not much face left, or paint. He's got a
sort of high black cap on. I should think they're Napoleonic, or
rather Wellington, being English. From what you can see of their
clothes."

"Well, *how* old, Daddy?" Max persisted.

"Well over a hundred years, if I'm right, Max. Take care of
them, do, I don't know that you ought to be allowed to play with
them."

"But I found them," Max exploded. And of course, because
they were admired and valued, Max had quickly become devoted to
them. Jane said they were shabby, and Philip said they were worm-
eaten (which was not true, it was only because he had not found
them himself). But Max adored them. One or two still had a round,
flat stand with two holes in it for their feet to go into. They were
not all the same size, some were taller than others, and although
their faces were blurred and rubbed, you could still tell that each
was different. Mrs. Morley said this was delightful because it
proved they were hand-made, each carved with his own face. Max
agreed.

But all this was as nothing to the time, two days ago, when he
had set them out on the attic floor, and lying on his tummy had
beat with his fingers on the Ashanti drum, so that they could march
to it. Before Max's startled eyes, one, a tallish fellow, at once
picked out by his sly, bird-like alertness, hopped and twirled into
life at the sound of the drum. He threw his tiny arms in the air as
if he were glad to feel life again, he skipped along the ranks, punching some in the jaw, tweaking the noses of others, and tripping the
feet of the most stolid. Then he found his place in line again and
the whole lot stood to surprised attention and took at least ten tiny
steps forward over the boards.

When Max half started to his feet in excitement, they stopped.
Froze, like a toad which freezes when you meet him crossing the
lawn. Even the lively fellow froze.

Then, today, he had heard their tiny noises and seen them at it.
Before Jane had come and spoiled everything.

So now he knew he must be gentle and careful and not do sudden
things. Max was a persistent boy, and patient for his age (which is

not a patient age) so he just sat there on the Ashanti stool, wondering if an Ashanti king had been crowned on it, and with his hands on his thin knees. He could wait as long as they could. They would trust him sooner or later. Surely they knew he loved them? . . . If he were an Ashanti king the first person he would sacrifice would be Anthony Gore. He knew that it was wrong to do human sacrifices, but then if he were an Ashanti king in those old days, he would *not* know this, so it would be all right. He supposed. When they knew better, they stopped doing it. Max wondered if they missed it very much.

Max sighed and tried smiling at the soldiers. Then he tapped with two fingers on the drum which stood beside him, the rhythm of a song. He started to sing it, almost in a whisper, so as not to frighten them:

> *"Oh, the brave old Duke of York,*
> *He had ten thousand men;*
> *He marched them up to the top of the hill*
> *And he marched them down again."*

It was the only marching song he could think of, about old soldiers.

> *"And when they were up, they were up,*
> *And when they were down, they were down,*
> *And when they were only half-way up,*
> *They were neither up nor down,"*

piped Max, very quietly, soft as a pin. To his joy the soldiers broke ranks, and clustered all together in a little band. Again he heard that faint crackling, whisking sound which was their talk. He was not surprised, this time, because he had been expecting it. He kept still.

One of them turned away from the rest and came boldly over the attic floor to Max. Behind him, prancing from side to side as if to urge him on, came the lively soldier Max had first seen move. He gave the other a good push at the last, but he seemed to be a stately and dignified character and did not lose his balance. Then they all bowed low from the waist, and the one in front lifted his arms and waggled his head.

The Patriarch

"Now, does he want me to pick him up?" Max wondered. Dare he? Would it frighten them?

He gently put out his hand, leaned down, and grasped the dignified little soldier by the waist. No bigger than that lizard he picked up the other day on the moor. The fellow waved his arms, but did not struggle.

Max brought him up to his face. He perhaps wanted to say something. He held him near to his ear. There was a crackle. Max closed his eyes and listened, very hard, holding his breath. The crackle came again, in more of a pattern. Max brought him a bit nearer. The third time, he could hear and understand.

"Are you one of the Genii?" said the creature.

Now Max had read the Arabian Nights, he knew all about the Genii, those spirits who preside over a person's destiny all his life. If these soldiers wanted him to be a Genii to them, he did not mind. So he said:

"Yes," very solemnly and quietly. He was surprised to hear a sudden faint sprinkle of sound like rice falling on the floor. It was the soldiers, clapping.

"I am Butter Crashey," said the small fellow he was holding. Max did not know what to say to this. Should he say how do you do? Or I like you very much? Or how old are you? Or where did you come from? None seemed quite right, and the last two seemed rude, so he said:

"I like your name. How did you get it?"

"I fell, long ago, into the butter," said his friend.

"I thought you must have," said Max.

"I am the patriarch of the Twelves," he went on, "and my age is one hundred and forty." Max had a vague idea that if a person were very old, it was proper to congratulate him. So he said:

"Good for you." Then he thought this sounded not old-fashioned enough, so he added:

"Allow me to congratulate you upon being full of years and wisdom."

This was the way Philip sometimes spoke. Max felt pleased with it, and so, it was clear, did Butter Crashey. He bent his head to receive the compliment. Now that he was alive, his face had become

15

sharp and detailed. It was not any longer blurred and featureless with being so old. It was like bringing a scene properly into focus through the field-glasses. Max looked at all the others, and saw that the same was true of them. The jaunty soldier seemed to have particularly piercing eyes, and he pulled a face as Max looked. Max was delighted.

"Under your protection," announced Butter Crashey next, "we propose to make a journey of discovery, as we once set forth under the four Genii to carve out a kingdom amongst the Ashanti."

"That is a very good idea," said Max, who was longing to see the soldiers moving about downstairs. He put the patriarch gently down with the rest, and went to the attic door. He opened it and stood to one side. The twelve soldiers formed into a column, marched towards the door, and out on to the landing.

Chapter 3

The
Perilous Descent

When they reached the fearful precipice of the stairs, they halted, broke out of their column and stood along the top step like people on top of a cliff. They waved their arms, peered over, nudged each other, pointed, consulted each with his neighbour, and then gathered round one who was taller than the rest. Max had noticed him before, he was good-looking and well-made and dashing. He might not be so old and wise as Butter Crashey, or so impulsive as the lively one, but he looked more of a leader. Max wondered if he had a name, too, and what it was.

But he did not want to interrupt their preparations.

They formed into a line again, and lay down, every man holding on to the ankles of the one ahead. The first was the tall leader, the last was the patriarch. But the leader was the other way round, holding the hands of the next, and facing him. Then he wriggled to the edge of the top stair, and began to drop carefully down, backwards. The steep attic stair was twice as tall as he. Before he had touched ground the man holding him was leaning well over but held safely by his ankles. The leader gave a small shout, let go the man's hands, and jumped, sprawling, on to the first stair.

"Well done," Max said to himself, as he saw the brave soldier recover his balance, and stand square against the perpendicular wall of the stair.

The next man then turned round, held the hands of the one behind him and was let over in the same way. But he landed upon the shoulders of the waiting leader, and then slipped down his back to the ground.

Max watched fascinated as each soldier in turn was lowered. But

17

what was going to happen to Butter Crashey? As it was, he was having difficulty in holding the last man without being tugged over. However, the patriarch, one hundred and forty though he was, turned round on his tummy, wriggled his legs over, and holding on to the top, lowered himself down. His legs waved, there was a shrill shrieking from the others, the jaunty soldier pranced with excitement, and then the patriarch found the shoulders of the tall leader. He was lifted down by the willing arms of all the rest.

But this was only one step. They now clustered at the brink of the next. Max could see their difficulty. There was not room for them to lie in a column and hold each other, this time. What they needed was a rope or a ladder.

"We shall be here all night," he said to himself, thinking.

He had an instinct that if he were to pick them all up, put them into the shoe box where he kept them, and carry them down, they might think it a terrible insult. They might freeze again at once, to pay him out. What he had to do was to suggest some better way and let them discover it.

He went into the attic and fetched the ball of string which was kept in the trunk of brown paper for parcels. He tied one end firmly on to the banister post, low down, so that if a soldier stood upon the slope the wooden railings were fitted into, he could hold on to it, and walk down the slope as if it were a ramp. Then he crept past the chattering soldiers down the stairs, with the string, every now and then putting it round a railing to keep it firm. Round the corner he went and down to the landing, doing two turns of string at the big posts, and so on, until he had made a hand rail down the two main flights to the hall. Then he pulled it firm, tied a good knot and cut it off the ball. All they had to do was to clamber up on to the slope from the stair. Surely they could help each other up, they seemed sensible and agile.

To his utter delight, he met the tall leader on the first landing, waiting at the foot of the slope as if he were taking the salute at a march past. Above him at different intervals came the rest. One ran down shouting a thin war cry. The next slid sideways, both hands on the rope and facing it. The third was sitting down as if he were on a sledge, his hand holding the rope above him. One

came down backwards. The lively one used the rope as a trapeze and swung with his feet drawn up, screaming a thin scream of glee. Max was enchanted. They were all different, like real people. He was only sorry he had missed seeing them notice their rope. He looked up, in time to see the venerable Butter Crashey heave the last man up to the ramp. But before the last man descended, he turned round, and holding the string to steady himself, he held out a hand to the patriarch and pulled him aloft.

"Hooray!" Max could not help saying. "You're all different. You're sensible, you think of each other, too." The patriarch marched solemnly down the slope, as befitted one so old, slow and upright. This he somewhat spoilt by slipping on the last lap, and landing on his back with his heels in the air. But so much did the rest respect him, that none laughed (except Max) and all gathered quickly to pick him up.

The delight of the Twelves, as the patriarch had called them, in finding that the rope went on all the way down, was lovely to see. Max tiptoed beside them (very softly) with great pleasure. They

made the descent more and more quickly, and with shouts of glee
and abandon the quicker they went, so that they sounded like a
miniature flock of whistling, calling, twittering birds in a copse
after rain.

And now what would they do? All the doors stood open, they
could turn into the dining-room or the drawing-room or the study;
they could march along to the kitchen; they could even snuff the
call of the open air from the front door which stood wide, and go
out into the sunlight.

At this minute the hot afternoon stillness was shattered by the
piercing ring of the telephone. As he hurried to answer it, Max
could not help watching the soldiers. They jumped as if they were
shot, and clustered into a crowd, holding their hands to their ears,
and looking up into the sky (or the ceiling).

Max reached the telephone, seized it and stopped its din.

"Hullo," he said. He had not learned the number yet, and he
was too startled to say anything else. He kept his eye on the
soldiers.

"Maxy?"

"Yes?"

"Are you all right, darling?"

"Yes, very."

"What are you doing?"

"Oh, mucking around."

"You were quite near the 'phone."

"Yes, I'm in the hall."

The Twelves had formed up, and were making for the drawing-
room.

"In the hall? Why don't you play in the garden?"

This was the kind of stupid question grown-ups always asked.

"Because I like being in the hall," Maxy said patiently. "Anyway, I'm going in the drawing-room now."

They had disappeared into the drawing-room. He was missing
all the fun, yet it was kind of his mother to ring him up.

"Have you had your tea?"

"Not yet, I haven't had time," Max said.

"When you have it, you can give Brutus his milk."

"Where is Brutus?" Max said, a sudden horrible thought striking him.

"Last seen by me in the green chair in the drawing-room," said his mother.

"Help. Well, good-bye, Mummy, I'm in the middle of something."

"Good-bye, darling, glad you're all right."

Max slammed the receiver back and hurried for the drawing-room. The soldiers were marching unsuspectingly over the carpet, letting out little sounds of amazement.

Brutus, woken by the telephone, had reared up in his chair, and was stretching, his back arched like a croquet hoop, the fur on his fat legs parting in flakes. He turned round, hearing Max, and saw them moving.

His ears went pointed, his whiskers were pushed forward, his mouth opened slightly, and he yickered as when he saw a bird near at hand.

"Brutus!" gasped Max. Brutus took a flying leap and landed smack on top of the moving soldiers.

"Oh help, help," Max said diving forward. "You've squashed them. You'll kill them, you beastly cat——" and he seized Brutus hastily and lifted him up. The soldiers, winded and terrified, fled in all directions. All except one limp form, who was clutched in the crook of Brutus's great white paw. Max gently detached him, put Brutus out and shut the door. The poor fellow was in a complete swoon, and no wonder. Max laid him on the carpet, and waited. Soon the noble Butter Crashey came out from under a chair, and the rest cautiously followed.

They ran to their companion and began to cheer him up. They lifted his head, and rubbed his hands.

"Take heart, Bravey, remember your own saying: 'Eat, drink and be merry, for tomorrow we die.' But you are not dead, I assure you."

"The Genii have protected you."

"Pray sit up and stop fainting," said the jaunty soldier, crossly, jealous of the attention the sufferer was getting.

"Give him air."

"Let Cheeky get at him! Let the stout-hearted doctor see him. Out of the way, Monkey."

"Stand back, Crackey and Tracky," said one who must have been the doctor.

Max saw the doctor make a few passes over the soldier called Bravey, feel his pulse, and rub his hands. Bravey came to, and blinked and sat up.

"Quite resuscitated," said Cheeky the doctor.

"Made alive," added the patriarch.

"Bring him some wine," suggested the tall leader.

"It little becomes the Duke to ask for wine in the wilderness," said one. Max crossed to the cupboard where his father kept the drinks. He took out the tiniest glass there was, meant for liqueurs, poured a drop of sherry into it, brought it over to the soldiers and said softly:

"The Genii can do anything, even bring wine in the desert."

They gathered round the glass with whoops of joy. They dipped Bravey's finger in, and made him suck it. He at once became more cheerful and talkative.

"Eat, drink and be merry," he squealed.

Soon they were all dipping their hands in and sucking, and the noise was considerable.

Chapter 4

The Duke
of Wellington

The sherry was certainly putting heart into the Twelves. The more they sucked the more noisy they became, and some began to shake their fists as if they meant battle. Max swooped down his finger and thumb, silently took the glass away and returned it to the cupboard. They looked for it for a little, but soon gave up and began to explore again. As they were so very brave and gay at the moment, he decided to risk picking one up. He chose the tall leader, whom somebody had called the Duke. The Duke looked a little amazed at feeling himself clutched and flying through the air, but he did not stiffen, he felt wriggly and lively like the lizard. Max put him down on the open piano and said softly:

"If your Grace likes to march along here it will be as good as a band." His Grace stepped on to a slippery white key, which gradually let him down and thundered out a deep note. Feeling himself going down, he held out his arms to keep his balance and strode quickly on from note to note up the scale, filling the drawing-room with a tinkle of music.

This seemed to excite the rest even more. Butter Crashey had led a small party towards the French window, where they were looking out to the garden with their hands against the glass. The person called Monkey had climbed up a pile of books waiting to be put away, had reached the swinging curtain cord, and was now swarming up it like a sailor. After him went the two who were called Crackey and Tracky, as if the cords were the rigging of a ship. As they climbed, the cord swung.

Meanwhile, poor Bravey, overcome first by Brutus and then by

The Duke of Wellington

the sherry, had stumbled as far as the white fur rug by the fireplace and was marching bravely over it like a man over a snowdrift, sinking up to his knees and often falling flat upon his face. As he scrambled up he was still saying, "Give us good cheer, eat, drink, dance and be merry," though his voice was certainly a little thick.

Max kept his eye on them all in turn, for he did not want to lose any. The Duke had reached the top of the scale, and was now skating back, making an exciting trill as he skimmed lightly over the notes.

Max decided that he was hungry and saw that it was tea-time. First, shutting the soldiers carefully into the drawing-room, he went out to the kitchen, took Brutus from the window-sill, and gave him his milk outside the back door. Then he fetched the cake and the buns and the loaf, the butter and jam, a large mug of milk and everything else he needed, and put them on to the kitchen table.

Now. He went back to the drawing-room. He did not want to pick everyone up without any warning, in case it frightened them and spoilt their fun. Added to this, the most interesting part of the affair was to see what they could arrange on their own.

He went over to Butter Crashey, who, with his few followers, was now watching the antics of Monkey, Crackey and Tracky on the curtain cord. The cord was swinging wildly. Monkey wanted to slide down, Tracky wanted to get to the top, and Crackey was caught like a pig in the middle. Monkey kicked him from above, Tracky butted him from below. The patriarch's men were standing at the bottom of the cord, urging on their favourites, and the noise was like a weasel fight.

The patriarch himself was trying to stop the quarrel and calm the fighters, by holding his arms up, clapping slowly and saying:

"Hush! Halt! Have done!" Max lifted up Crashey, as he still said "halt", and whispered: "I want you all to come into the kitchen. How can we collect everyone?"

The patriarch looked at him a moment with his mouth open and then replied, "Without doubt, the Duke must blow his trumpet. This is what he always did, when he was a humble trumpeter, and the Twelves obeyed. Tell him to do this, and see what follows."

24

The Duke of Wellington

"But he hasn't got a trumpet," Max said.

"No, he has become too grand since he was Duke," said the patriarch.

"What is he duke of?" said Max.

"He is Arthur Wellesley, Duke of Wellington," said Butter Crashey, solemnly, "which honour came to him after the famous battle of Waterloo. But perhaps you do not know about Waterloo?"

"I know all about Waterloo," Max said. "I'll tell him to tootle without a trumpet."

Still carrying Crashey, he went over to the piano.

"The patriarch commands your Grace to collect the Twelves," explained Max.

The Duke stopped dead on middle C, and lifted his empty hands in despair. However, the tootle he produced from his own small throat was bold, piercing and commanding (it reminded Max of a bird's whistle) and before he had finished Max saw the soldiers gathering.

He put the patriarch on the carpet, lifted down the Duke of Wellington, and helped Bravey out of his jungle. Tracky slid down the curtain cord, followed quickly by the others, and soon the whole band was marshalled behind the Duke and marching towards the kitchen.

Max lifted them gingerly one by one on to the kitchen table, and was pleased to see that they did not seem to mind. Then he sat down to enjoy his tea and watch what they would do at the same time.

They marched all round the kitchen table as if to make sure where they were. Then they came nearer to Max's end, and walked round the bread board, pointing up at the loaf as if it were a hillock. They showed great interest in the butter, too, all the more when Max cut a piece off and carried it to his own plate.

Then they gathered round his plate, sat in a circle, and watched each mouthful he took.

"Like Brutus," Max said. "I bet you're hungry."

He gave each man a large crumb of bread, followed by a smaller crumb of cake, and they ate them with relish.

"Tell me about your famous expedition to carve out your

kingdom amongst the Ashanti," Max said. "I know it is ignorant of me not to have heard of it," he added, "but I am only eight."

"Crackey is only five," remarked a grave-looking soldier whom Max had not noticed much before, "and *he* has heard of it."

"Of course he's heard of it if he went on it," argued Max, rather rudely. And the whole lot threw back their heads and laughed at the grave soldier, who looked sourer than ever. The jaunty one even pointed and jeered.

"You are answered, Gravey," said the Duke.

"Why is he called Gravey?" asked Max. "Did he fall in the gravy, or is it to rhyme with Bravey?"

"Both," said several soldiers, thoughtlessly.

"Neither," said Butter Crashey. "He is grave and melancholy, so his name is naturally Gravey."

"I say, Gravey," began Max, seeing the poor fellow scowling and drawing his brows together. "I am sorry I answered you back. Please tell me about the expedition."

The soldiers began to twitter, and those next to the patriarch nudged him with their elbows.

The Duke of Wellington

The patriarch swallowed his last crumb of cake, cleared his throat, and began to speak.

"We set out in a ship called the *Invincible*," he said. "I was the captain, Cheeky was the surgeon, and the most stout-hearted man in the ship. The rest were trumpeters and sailors, and those fellows you saw climbing the rope were middies. After many adventures, including storms, and battles with enemies, we reached Africa, fought the Ashanti, and began to build our first town——"

At this minute there was a loud engine noise in the yard, the doors of the motor-car slammed, footsteps ran towards the house, voices yelled and called, and the back door, which Max had carefully closed to keep Brutus out, was flung open with a whoop by Jane.

The effect of all this noise was horrifying. The Twelves scattered in all directions. Several ran to the edge of the table and fell hurtling to the ground. The lively one bumped against the bread board and went flat on his face at the foot of bread hill, lying as if he were stunned. Some simply swooned where they were and slumped as if dead. The patriarch stumbled over the butter dish, fell head first, and was caught by his head and fists in the soft mound.

"Here he is, here he is!" shrieked Jane.

Max, scarlet in the face with rage and fright, dived under the table to rescue the fallen. There was no time to be polite or gentle. He seized them up, counting as he went. One had crawled towards the stove, and Jane's foot was nearly on him.

"Look OUT," yelled Max.

"All right," she said crossly. "What is it? What's the matter?"

"Eight, nine," muttered Max, standing up, his hair over his eyes. "Ten," he said, seizing the greasy Butter Crashey, "eleven," he added, tenderly rescuing the little soldier on the bread board.

"Eleven," said Max, worried.

"Eleven what? What are you doing? Oh, those dirty old soldiers."

"Shut up," said Max.

"Don't be so cross, Maxy dear, here we all are. What is it?"

"You're back much earlier than you said," Max scowled.

"We didn't say," said Mr. Morley. "Let's have some tea."

"Yes, come on. Move up, Max, and we'll lay it properly," said his mother, dumping her parcels.

"Our little man seems upset," remarked Philip. "I'm ravening," he said, taking a bun.

"I've had my tea," Max said with dignity, clutching his soldiers to his chest, "and there's one of the Twelves missing, so please don't tread on him. *Please.* He's here somewhere."

"The twelves?" Mrs. Morley said, putting the kettle on. "What is the twelves?"

"The soldiers. The old soldiers."

"Oh well, find it, and rescue it, darling."

"I don't know where he's gone."

"You've put him down somewhere, he hasn't *gone.*"

"He *has* gone," said Max, stubbornly. And he turned and went out of the kitchen and tramped slowly up the stairs.

He could feel what had happened. They were all stiff and wooden in his hands, they were frozen. He laid them into their box and their faces were blurred and old again.

"Oh, do come back soon, don't freeze for ever, please, please don't. I want to hear about the expedition," Max whispered.

Chapter 5

The Brontyfan

Where he had gone to was a mystery, that missing soldier. Max had spent the whole of the next morning hunting. He had looked so thoroughly in the kitchen and the pantry and the larder that he had made his mother suspicious.

"But, Max, you didn't *play* in the pantry or the larder, did you? How could it have got there?"

It was no good saying that the fellow had walked. But this was the fact: he could have walked, unless he were wounded or dead with his fall. And in this case Max would have found him on the floor.

"Well, I went in to get my tea. My cake and bread and things," Max said, slyly.

"Oh, I see. Did you go into the garden?"

"No."

"Because I don't think it's in here. Mrs. Hodgson has cleaned this, she'd have found it."

"Mummy, she couldn't have thrown him away? In the dustbin, or *on the fire*? Could she?" Max said suddenly, with horror.

"You can look in the dustbin. But I don't think she would, she'd see it was a soldier. I'll mention it to her. And, Maxy, while I think of it, must we have that piece of string tied all down the banisters?"

"Yes, I need it monstrously," Max said, using a word of Philip's.

His mother laughed.

"What for, darling? It looks awful. And how can Mrs. Hodgson polish?"

"It's an important game. I can't keep taking it off. Anyway, she doesn't polish that slope the rails are in."

"Indeed she does. I hope."

"Well, I hope she doesn't. It'll make it so slippery."

"But nobody walks on the slope!"

"Oh, don't they," Max muttered.

"What? You're not to play capers with the banisters, Max. You're certainly not to climb down outside, there's too far to fall."

"I wasn't going to."

"Philip tried it once at the other house."

"Did he?" Max said with interest. "I didn't know."

"Max," said his father at this minute, coming in from the drawing-room where he had been giving the parson some sherry, "don't help yourself to sherry, old boy, it's too expensive."

"I didn't, I——"

"What's this, then?" Mr. Morley held up the little liqueur glass, with sherry in the bottom.

"Oh, yes. I borrowed a little," Max said, grinning.

"Max! Did you like it?" asked his mother.

"I didn't drink it, it was just a game," Max said.

"You can play games with water. And not the best glasses," said his father.

"No, I needed sherry. Monstrously," Max said, as he slipped out of the kitchen.

"He's lost that old soldier, Roderick. Will you keep a look-out for it?" said Mrs. Morley.

"I said he oughtn't to be allowed to play with them. They should be in the drawing-room cabinet," said her husband.

"That seems so useless, doesn't it? He adores them."

"I say, this parson's an absolute Brontë fan. Are you coming in?"

"Yes, in half a minute. Of course, we're next door now, aren't we?" she replied, as her husband hurried out. Max came back, his small dwarf face looking puzzled.

"What's a brontyfan?" he said.

"I'll tell you later, darling, I must go and say how do you do to the parson," said his mother.

Brontyfan, Max muttered, walking up the stairs towards the

attic. For he might as well go and see. Once more. His heart was heavy, because it was two days. Was it perhaps because one was lost? Were they hurt in their feelings that he, the Genii, had not protected the twelfth? Brontyfan. It couldn't be that enormous prehistoric creature in the museum, although that was a bronty something, he knew. But no parson could be one of those. Unless his father meant he looked like it? Perhaps he had a huge, long neck? Brontyfan. And also, what were we next door to? It sounded as if we were next door to its lair.

Max could hear Philip singing, practising his funny, cracking voice, he supposed.

> *"Brave Benbow lost his legs, by chain-shot, by chain-sho-o-ot,*
> *Brave Benbow lost his legs, by chain-shot,*
> *Brave Benbow lost his legs, and all on his stumps he begs,*
> *Fight on my English lads, 'tis our lot, 'tis our lot,"*

roared Philip. And then Max heard the drum. Ti tum tiddle um tum tum. Tum ti tum tum ti tum. He was beating the Ashanti drum! Max flew up the last flight. He had suddenly remembered what happened when last he beat the drum! Why had he forgotten to try this? It was natural after all, since they had once been on this expedition to Africa and fought the Ashanti, that his great-grandfather's drum should make them excited.

> *"Let a cradle now in haste on the quarter deck be placed,*
> *That the enemy I may face till I die, till I die,"*

sang Philip again. And he beat an absolute tattoo upon the drum to finish off. The attic door was open, Max stood breathing gustily and gazing at Philip. And from Philip, he looked furtively to the corner of the attic. The far corner. Where they all were. He had arranged them, hopefully, in rows. They were moving.

He looked quickly away.

"What's up with you?" Philip said. "Seen a ghost?"

Max moved quickly between Philip and the soldiers. He did not want to lose his secret. Not yet.

"Why are you playing the drum?" Max said.

The Brontyfan

"Why shouldn't I? You haven't got a monopoly of this drum," said his brother.

"I say, Phil," Max began hastily, "what's a brontyfan?"

Philip was silent a moment: and then he roared with laughter.

"Don't you know?" he teased.

Max's only thought was to get him out of the attic. He did not care about this stupid brontyfan, it could be what it liked.

"What do you *think* it is?" went on Philip, teasing him.

"Well, this parson's one, or like one I suppose, and he's in the drawing-room and I expect they want you to go down, so can you go and say how do you do, quickly, you might get some sherry," Max said, adding this as a bait.

"You come too," said Philip, bounding up from the Ashanti stool, "and we'll have a nice joke about Brontë fans. Come on, Maxy."

"No, I'm busy," Max said, tugging his sleeve away from Philip.

"Cowardy," said his brother thundering down the stairs.

Max breathed again, and shut the attic door. Then he crept to the stool and sat down. They had not got far. They were coming. Max's pointed face spread into a slow smile. Butter Crashey, the Duke of Wellington, and then a gap; on they came in four rows of three this time. Gravey, Bravey and Cheeky; then the three whose names Max had not yet learned, one of them the fellow who had roused all the others the first time. Last, the young and wild middies who climbed the curtain cord, Monkey, Tracky and Crackey. The gap was the missing soldier. Max could hardly bear to look at it. They halted, and the patriarch moved out. He went solemnly along the rows, pointing at each man. He pointed at himself, last, and scratched his head. Then the Duke did the same. A great burst of chattering arose as they broke ranks.

"Oh, they're counting," Max said. It was clear they had realized there was a man short. Then they gathered in a band, and all began saying the same thing. Louder and louder came the chant, until Max was able to hear what it was, even from his end of the attic.

The Brontyfan

"Frederic Guelph, Duke of York!
Frederic the First, King of the Twelves!
After that, became Frederic the Second!
Otherwise known to us as Stumps!
Stumps! Stumps! Where is Stumps?"

"Now I know who is lost," Max said to himself. "His nickname is Stumps."

Butter Crashey left the group of chanting soldiers and came towards Max. Max bent down and picked him gently up.

"I have come to consult you, oh Genii," he began, "because Stumps is lost again."

"Oh, has he been lost before?" said Max.

"Yes, indeed, he was lost upon Ascension Island on the way to Africa. He was killed by the enemy. When the rest searched for him to make him alive, he had disappeared." Max was glad to hear that they could make each other alive. This was splendid. No wonder they had lasted so many years.

"And what was his real name?" he asked the patriarch, thinking of the chant he had just heard.

"The history of Stumps is long, complicated and shrouded in mystery," said Butter Crashey. "He was two people, and only the Genii know why, they decreed it. As Stumps, he was lost on the way to Africa. But he was also Frederic Guelph, Duke of York." Max was pleased that there really was a Duke of York amongst them, and he began to sing his song.

"Oh, the brave old Duke of York,
He had ten thousand men;
He marched them up to the top of the hill,
And he marched them down again,"

sang Max in a tiny voice. The patriarch was evidently delighted with this compliment. He was balanced upon Max's left hand, and he tramped up and down his arm, as Max sang, as if he were climbing the hill, and coming down again. He felt like a sparrow on Max's bare skin.

"Go on about the Duke of York," Max said.

"As to the Duke of York, he was elected King of the Young Men, and became Frederic the First."

"Who were the Young Men?" Max said next.

"Why, we are the Young Men," Butter replied, drawing himself up. Max did not like to remind him that he was one hundred and forty, so he simply said:

"I thought you said you were called the Twelves."

"We are called both."

"Why?" said Max. Butter Crashey thought a moment.

"It is a sign of low birth and no spirit to have but one name," he said. "You yourself are sometimes the Genii, sometimes Max." Max smiled.

"I didn't know you knew I was Max," he said.

"I have heard the name in the air," said the patriarch, waving his little thin arm.

"Well, go on about Frederic the First."

"Alas, he was killed in the first battle with the Ashantis. He was killed so as he could not be got alive. He was the best monarch that ever sat upon the throne of the Twelves," Butter sighed.

"If he was killed so as he could not be got alive," Max said puzzled, "why is he still here? Because he was, till he got lost again."

"Ah, but I have told you, he was two people," went on the patriarch. "He was Stumps, remember, as well as the Duke. One day I heard a hollow, tomb-like voice, calling Crashey! Crashey! I went out and returned with a ghastly, skeleton-like figure, clothed in tarnished regimentals. It was poor Stumps, come back from Ascension Island."

What marvellous stories he tells, thought Max.

"I see," he said. He saw perfectly well.

This was absolutely what happened with soldiers. They did change names, they died, were made alive, got lost, turned up again, and became someone else.

"Whereupon," said B. Crashey solemnly, "I said, 'Young Men, elect him for your king. All know his courage, coolness, integrity, ability.' So they did. He became Frederic the Second. He was a good king; though his qualities were not shining, yet they were of sterling worth."

"But isn't he still king? What happened next?" Max asked. For the Twelves seemed to have a complete history, like any other people.

"The last act of his reign was the best," said Butter Crashey. "When the Duke of Wellington, scourge of Napoleon, returned to Ashanti from the battle of Waterloo and told us all his brave deeds, Frederic the Second arose, and took the crown off his head, and placed it on that of the Duke of Wellington, saying, 'I am not worthy to rule this man, he is your king'. " And the patriarch held his arms up and removed an imaginary crown in the air.

No wonder, thought Max, that the Duke is now the leader. He could not help feeling sorry for Stumps, thus demoted from being king; but this was, again, just what happened with soldiers, favourites were made and then they fell. As if in answer to his thought the patriarch said wisely:

"If you want my opinion, he preferred being Stumps to being king. He was free and he liked adventures. So it is not altogether surprising that he is lost again," he went on, "but if you will tell me, as oracle, where to look, I will send out a search party."

Max frowned and considered. He did not know where Stumps was. But as Genii, he did not like to say so. It would not do for Butter Crashey, who said he was their oracle, which Max thought meant a kind of prophet, to go back to the Twelves and say the Genii did not know. Anyway, Max knew the rules of this game. What the Genii did not know or had not considered, they must make up. He must even find another soldier, if Stumps was gone for ever.

"I myself am searching for your king," he said solemnly, "if he does not return, consult me again." And with this oracular remark, Butter seemed satisfied.

Chapter 6

Stumps

"Who were you talking to?" said Jane, standing outside the attic door. Max had thought he heard someone, but Jane was so light, she crept about like a small wind; or it might be the wood of the old stairs creaking for no reason. Then there had been a little shuffle. He had quickly put the patriarch down with the rest and gone to the attic door. Jane looked sheepish and she was smiling. Max came out, shut the door behind him, and said:

"You shouldn't have been listening."

"It sounded interesting. Was it your game with your soldiers? Maxy, I wish you'd let me play, I like your games."

Max looked at Jane, considering. It was perfectly true that he and she had often made up wonderful games that went on for days. Jane was a good maker-up of games and she did not let secrets out, usually. But lately she had played much less with Max, and spent much more time reading on her own. Max had thought she was getting too old to like made-up games, just as Philip had done.

Jane had eyes the colour of speedwells, and they were now fixed on Max, trying to understand the look on his face. Her features were pale and pointed, rather like Max's, but what looked all right on a boy was not pretty enough for a girl. Jane's one beauty was her eyes.

"I like the weeny voice you do for them to answer in," she said next. "I could hardly hear it, it sounded so whispery, but it went on quite a long time. How do you do it without moving your lips?"

"How do you know I don't move my lips? Jane, you're an eavesdropper *and* an eyedropper, you must have looked through

36

the keyhole." Jane laughed a shrill laugh which was like her mother's.

"There's no such word as an eyedropper," she said.

"There is if I say so," said Max. "Anyway, you must have been," he accused her.

"Yes, I was. I couldn't hear the words very well, except something about searching, so I bet it's that soldier you've lost. Come on, Max, you've got to shake hands with this parson."

"That old brontyfan," scowled Max.

"How did you know he was a Brontë fan?"

"Heard Daddy say so. What does it mean, by the way?" Max asked, as casually as he knew how and as if he did not care at all. This, he had learned, was the only way to find things out and at the same time not lose face. It might work with Jane, though older people like Philip always saw through it. Grown-ups saw through it too, but kindly pretended they had not, and explained.

"It's someone who's mad on the Brontës. You know, fan like in fan-mail. For instance," Jane went on kindly as they marched downstairs side by side, Max hanging on to her waist, "if you're cracked on a film star,"—Jane was—"then you're a fan of his."

But this was not Max's main problem. He knew about fans, now that he knew it was a separate word.

"But what ARE bronties?" he said, hoping that Jane would go on being kind and not laugh.

"*The* Brontës. It's a family. They lived at Haworth. You know, it's quite near. And they were all so famous that it's a museum, the house they lived in. This parson has been telling us about it."

"What were they famous at?"

"They all wrote books. *Jane Eyre's* the best book I've ever read," Jane said in a deep and glowing tone, which her shrill voice took on when she was moved. "I've just finished it."

"Oh, is that the one with that mad woman shut up in it?" Max asked with interest. He had heard Jane talking about it.

"Yes, surely you knew it was by Charlotte Brontë."

"No, I didn't. What's this parson like?"

"All right. Nice."

Max liked him at once, because he was perfectly serious.

Stumps

"How do you do, Max. I'm interested to hear about your soldiers that you found," he said, shaking hands.

"Who told you?" Max said, shaking firmly in return.

"Your mother."

"I've lost one, but he'll come back," Max said.

"I'm sure he will. May I see them sometime?"

Max gazed at him. But he was still perfectly serious, he was not being patronizing.

"Maxy, Mr. Howson is very interested in old things and knows a lot about them."

"Butter's a hundred and forty," Max said without thinking.

"What, darling?"

"When I've found the lost one, you could. Perhaps," Max said quickly to Mr. Howson.

"Thank you. Very much. I shall remember." Max grinned at Mr. Howson, his wide mouth like a crescent moon above his pointed chin. He was in fact thinking of Mr. Howson's face if he saw them move. Mr. Howson grinned back. He was about forty-five, and he was tall and square-faced and black-browed and slightly tortured-looking when he did not smile. Waving at them all, he bicycled away.

"I know, he's like Mr. Rochester!" said Jane at lunch. "Mr. Howson."

"Yes, he is a bit," said her mother.

"I *adore* Mr. Rochester," said Jane.

"Oh, Jane," said Philip, wriggling sentimentally and pulling a face.

"Who's Mr. Rochester?" said Max.

"In *Jane Eyre*," said Jane.

"Pooh, these old Brontës," said Max, with dignity.

"Oh, so you've discovered," Phil said. "You know what, Mummy, he thought Mr. Howson was a kind of animal like a brontysaurus. Because of Brontë fan. Didn't you, Max? Own up! Eh?"

How did Philip know? How did he know so exactly? It was absolutely thought-reading. Max scowled and then giggled, cramming in his potato.

Stumps

But where was Stumps? Max lay in bed that night, wondering. He had had another search in the afternoon, he had even gone round the yard and the garden, with no success. When his mother had lost something, she always went very carefully over what could have happened. Max lay watching the creeper leaves which trimmed his window. They were rustly and green and it was not dark yet. The window was a square of pale green light like water.

What would Stumps have done, finding himself in the kitchen? What could he have done, Max wondered, following his mother's example. He must think of all the things he could have done. First, he must have crawled quickly away somewhere to hide. It must have been a very good place, for Max not to find him, nor yet Mrs. Hodgson when she cleaned. He might have moved about while she cleaned, keeping out of her way.

Then, what would he try to do? He was a valiant and sensible soldier, according to Butter Crashey, and used to adventures. He would certainly try to climb back to the attic, to join the rest, as he had once struggled back from Ascension Island. He would not forget their exciting descent. He would wait until the kitchen door was left open, and no huge and frightening people were about. Surely this is what he would do. This meant he would have to wait till night time.

But at night the kitchen door was never left open, because of Brutus. Stumps would come out to reconnoitre, and find himself shut in. Max thought of Stumps going round, trying to find a way out of the kitchen and into the hall. Round and round he would go, feeling and peering and tapping and grumbling. He would probably spend the whole night so. No window would be open even if he could climb as far.

And now Max seemed to see him, as if he were really in the kitchen watching. Stump's small arms were held up, exploring round the kitchen walls, looking for holes, like a prisoner in a cell. He reached the crack where the door was, but it was fast shut. He came to the great warm white boiler which heated the water, and went round behind it and came out the other side. And next to it the built-in cooker, and all along below the window where there were built-in cupboards. But they were no good to Stumps. And round the corner again to where the sink was. Stumps pushed behind the plastic curtains which hung all round below the sink and the draining-boards, and his heart beat because he thought he was getting out. But no, his hopes were dashed, it was solid wall at the back. And then he came to the refrigerator, and explored round it. Here was another door, and he could smell a slight smell of fresh air beyond it, but it was shut. It was not dark, the window panes were light. First they were light with moonlight. But later, as Stumps sat down worn out with his wandering, he saw them grow light with daylight. He tried to climb the table leg, but fell back, exhausted. He tried to swarm up the plastic curtain, but it was so slippery he could not hold on. He sat below the sink, and had he not been Frederic both the First and the Second, King of the Twelves, he would have cried. He found that by climbing on a great brush and a pile of soap powder packets he could just reach the bend in the pipe below the sink. He heaved himself up, and wedged safely in the bend he fell asleep.

No wonder I did not find him, thought Max. And the next night he would try again, he thought. Max did not know whether he were dreaming or imagining, by now. The next night, Stumps had better luck: the door into the scullery was open a crack, and beyond this, as he stumbled along over the stone tiles, he saw moonlight. He came at last to a little door, only about three times his size, curved in a noble arch above his head. It was a strange door, because it did not open right to the ground but seemed to be cut in the wall more like a window. It was Brutus's cat door, by which he hopped in and out. Stumps heaved himself up and over, and dropped down into the outside world! He was in the yard, but he was no nearer to the stairs, and the long climb up to the attic. It seemed that he was further away. He looked about him, bewildered in the bright light of the moon. He began to walk slowly over the yard. . . .

Max felt the full moon looking at him, opened his eyes, and remembered all he had seen or dreamed or imagined, about Stumps. Stumps! By now Stumps was making his way over the yard. Max leapt out of bed, as if he were sure of this, and looked out of his window.

Stumps

How diamond-bright the moon was! It looked cold, it was so bright. But the summer night was not cold, only slightly chilly. The moon cast shadows as dark as charcoal. Each cobble of the path to the farmyard had a light side and a black side. The nasturtiums round the water-butt and the creeper leaves below Max's window threw dark stencils on the flagstones. It was so arresting to see the bright middle of a moonlight night for almost the first time, as Max was doing, that for a minute or two he forgot why he was looking. He looked all round the yard, at the garage and the old stable and the sheds, and beyond to the pig-garden. He would never forget what he saw and the sounds and smells that went with it.

Something moved in the middle of the yard, a small creature casting a small shadow. If it were a mouse, the shadow would not be so thin. So it must be Stumps. This was no more than Max had expected. The tiny figure had now stopped, and Max found it difficult to keep his eye upon him, he was so small in the distance. What would he be doing? He would be looking up at the house, seeing how he could climb in, perhaps. This was what he, Max, would do if he were shut out.

Max noticed then, for the first time, that the great creeper which went past his window went on up to the attic. If Stumps were to climb it he would be all right. But if the moon made him mad for wandering, and he took it into his head to go exploring the pig-garden, Max might never find him again.

Taking a last look at Stumps to place him, he crept out of his room, down the stairs, and through the kitchen. He unbolted the back door and stepped out into the moon. His sharp eyes searched the yard. There he was. It was certainly Stumps, standing still, his shadow like a little clothes peg. He wondered whether it felt terrifying to be so little in such a huge world, under such an enormous moon-washed sky! Max thought of all the other small creatures, mice, toads, beetles, some much tinier than Stumps, ants and spiders and furry caterpillars. No doubt to God, he, Max, seemed quite as small and needing help. He felt he would like to protect all the creatures, and wondered who did. His job now was to protect Stumps.

Stumps

Max felt so pleased that Stumps was found that he was about to hurry over and swoop upon him, and carry him up to his safe attic. It seemed so easy to do this and surely the poor Duke of York (as he used to be), had suffered enough hardships.

But then he had a great longing to see if Stumps would manage for himself, would notice the creeper, and be able to climb that twisty thick trunk up to his window! There he could take him in and rescue him.

Even as Max was thinking all this, Stumps began to hurry towards the creeper. Max watched him until he could not tell Stumps from the pointed leaves into which he had dived. Then he hurried back to his room and leaned out of the window.

Far below him he could hear a rustle, a scrape and a shiver in the creeper. The sounds came slowly closer, and closer, a shuffle and a ruffle of leaves. Then Max thought he could make out a thin, breathless tune.

"Boney was a warrior . . ." then a long pause. Then a little grunt, as he found a foothold. "Boney was a warrior. . . ." Then very slowly as the singer wriggled himself on his front up the trunk, "way . . . yay . . . yah". Then more briskly, as he swung from twig to twig on his feet:

> *"Boney was a warrior*
> *John France wah!*
> *Boney beat . . . the Rooshians*
> *Way—ay—yah*
> *Boney beat the Rooshians,*
> *John France—wah!"*

Then a long, scrambling pause, and the singer started again.

> *"Boney went to Mossycow . . .*
> *Way—ay—yah*
> *Boney he came back again*
> *John France—wah!*
> *Woops!"*

A tiny slither and a breathless gasp. Then the thin voice rose braver than before, and nearer.

> *"Boney went to Waterloo*
> *Way—ay—*YAH
> *Boney went to Waterloo*
> *John France—wah!"*

shouted the singer lustily.

But when Boney broke his heart and died, Max heard Stump's voice as plaintive as a humming gnat below him.

Nearer he climbed until at last Max saw the leaves twitch close at hand, and he stepped out into the moon, upon the piece of straight trunk trained past Max's window.

Max knew he must be discreet and gentle now, or he would frighten him and make him topple off into the yard.

"Well done, Stumps, once King of the Twelves," he whispered: and he put his hand very quietly out and grasped him. "The Genii has you in his hand."

Stumps must have understood, for he neither struggled nor went wooden. Max looked at Stumps closely for the first time in the moonlight. His main oddities were his round, turnipy head, and his stumpy, rather bandy legs. Max smiled, he loved Stumps. He carried him up the attic stairs, opened the door, and put him down upon the highway of moonlight which led to his companions.

Chapter 7

The Four Kings of Ashanti

Max woke up with a sense of excitement and remembered in a flash all about the return of Stumps. He swung out of bed.

"Stumps, Stumps, good old Stumps," he chanted, like the soldiers, flinging on his clothes. "Frederic Guelph (I think that's what they said, what a queer name) . . . Frederic Guelph, Duke of York, Frederic the First, Frederic the Second. I wonder if all the time underneath he really wished he could go on being king when he gave his crown to that old Duke of Wellington?"

Max sat on the bed, doing up his sandals, and he suddenly thought:

"I wonder who made all this up? Because they know all sorts of things about themselves, they know their names and their ages and all about going to Africa. Could they make it all up themselves? Butter could, perhaps, but no, I don't think so. I think it's the Genii who have to make things up. Like I do. Like I did about Stumps wandering round the kitchen and getting out of Brutus's door. And then it was really true, he really had."

It did not seem odd to Max that what he had imagined about Stumps was really true, because this was exactly how the games you made up worked. Of course they were true. In your mind. It was only that this had gone one step more and come alive, and he could watch it.

"All that about Ashanti and Africa," he muttered. "That would need a Genii. And I didn't make that up. There must have been another Genii, and I expect it was some boy who had them before. Before someone hid them under the floor board."

45

Max wondered who this boy was, so long ago. Over a hundred years ago, his father had said. Then he remembered that Butter Crashey had said, before they came downstairs, that they had gone to Africa under the protection of the four Genii. Four. Then were there *four* boys? Or there might have been some girls? After all, he would not mind Jane playing, she would make a good Genii, she loved making things up. Perhaps these old boys of a hundred years ago had a sister. Max determined he would ask the patriarch the next time he had the chance about the four Genii who used to protect them.

They would all know that he had searched for and protected Stumps and guided him back. He was longing to go and see them, but there was not time before breakfast. Max had overslept, after his wakeful night.

He ran down to the dining-room and flumped into his place. He was not quite last, he and Philip had a battle on the stairs, and he, Max, won.

"What a noise, boys," Mrs. Morley said.

"Noise boys boise noys noise boise," yelled Max. He felt fine.

"You seem full of beans," said his father. "What is it?"

"Stumps is found, by the way," said Max.

"Who's Stumps?" asked Jane.

"My wooden soldier."

"Oh, good, Maxy, I am relieved," his mother said. "Mr. Howson thinks they may be really valuable. So let that teach you to look after them."

"My whole life," said Max solemnly, "is going to be given up to protecting them."

"I hope your whole life won't be spent in the attic, darling. It's such lovely weather. You've been stuffing in there ever since you found them."

"Well, I like being with them."

"Bring them down, into the garden."

Max considered this in silence.

"What did you call him, Stumps?" said Philip, having satisfied his hunger a little with three large spoonfuls of cornflakes.

"Yes."

46

"Why?"

"Why not? Because he's got stumpy legs, I expect."

"And all on his stumps he begs," roared Philip, down the scale.

"Not at table," said Mr. Morley.

"He's got lots of other names anyway."

"Have they all got names?" said Jane.

"Yes, but I don't know them all."

"You mean you haven't thought of enough," she said. This was not what Max meant, but he did not say so.

"One's Butter, isn't it?" Philip said.

"How d'you know?" said Max.

"I heard you say it to Mr. Howson. I distinctly heard you say Butter's a hundred and forty. I blushed for your childish imaginings," said Philip. "But Mr. Rochester didn't notice."

Mr. Howson had become Mr. Rochester to them all. Jane was looking forward to going to church in order to stare at him again.

By the time Max was free to go up to the attic, after doing his jobs, it was nearly mid-morning. Philip had gone off over the purpling moors on his bicycle. Jane had disappeared somewhere or other, his mother was safely in the kitchen cooking, and talking to Mrs. Hodgson, his father was in the stackyard. He hoped very much that his mother would not return to her idea of his bringing Butter and Co. down: because he could not safely do this yet. Anybody might see them, and then the secret would be out, the excitement of having it for himself over. Or what was worse to contemplate, they might laugh and disbelieve, and then the precious wooden soldiers might freeze for ever. Max thought this was quite possible. Moreover, he did not yet know when they would freeze, or when they would not. They might flee, as they had done off the kitchen table. It was dangerous. So he must play with them up here, even though it was hot and sunny and he would have liked to go with Phil, to explore their new neighbourhood. He had brought a little pale blue flag on a pin, from a flagday collection. It seemed suitable for the soldiers.

He approached the attic quietly and saw to his surprise that the door was slightly open. Could he have left it unlatched last night, when he put Stumps back? If so it was careless of him, and dangerous. Supposing they had all trooped down to the hall, and been trodden on?

Max pushed the door quietly open. He was delighted to see that the soldiers were already on the move. Something important seemed to be afoot. So they did not always need the drum to rouse them. Perhaps, Max thought, the more he did with them the more active they would be. After all, they had been out of practice for over a hundred years, he supposed.

He crept in, closed the door, and then saw that he could not take his usual place on the Ashanti stool, because they were gathered round it. Max put the flag down near the stool and then squatted very quietly on the floor where he was and watched. The patriarch seemed to be directing operations. He was leading a small band of men over to the pile of balsa wood which Philip used to make things. Max looked at the soldiers.

"Those are Monkey, Crackey and Tracky, the midshipmen," he said to himself. These three, with Butter to help, ranged themselves each side of a long thin strip of balsa, picked it up as Butter said "Heave!" and began to carry it over towards the Ashanti stool.

They tramped past Max, panting heavily. They heaved the plank up so that it led like a ramp on to the Ashanti stool, and at this point Bravey, Gravey and Cheeky were there to help.

They're trying to climb on to it, Max thought. And then he remembered about the Kings of Ashanti being crowned on it: and wondered if this was why they wanted to climb on. He could see Stumps, sitting on the floor and leaning nonchalantly against the wall of the Ashanti canoe, with his short legs crossed.

Meanwhile in another group, evidently waiting for action, was the Duke of Wellington himself, or rather the King, as Max now knew. With the Duke was the lively, jaunty soldier who had first woken the rest to life, and whose name Max wanted badly to find out. The two other nameless soldiers were also there, chatting to the Duke and looking haughty and important. As Max watched, the jaunty fellow flung out his arms, pointed his toe, and put his head on one side, as if he were acting a part. "Perhaps I shall find out who they are this time," Max thought.

The ramp was now in position, held by six men. At the patriarch's word, three left it and hurrying over to Max's old bricks with which he sometimes made forts, they got behind one, and pushed it across the floor to hold firm the end of the ramp.

"Jolly good idea," Max said. "Now what happens?" What happened was that the Duke of Wellington scrambled on to the ramp, and began the perilous ascent to the Ashanti stool. "Goodness, he'll never do it," Max muttered.

The balsa wood was very smooth and slippery. The poor Duke slipped and scrambled up his improvised gangway, often going down upon his knees, and barely saving himself.

"This won't do," Max said, "for a King." And he began to sing, very softly, the Duke of York's song.

> *"And when he was up, he was up*
> *And when he was down he was down*
> *And when he was only half-way up*
> *He was neither up nor down,"*

Max sang, strictly in time, to a brisk rhythm. The Duke seemed to take heart, stood up, held out his arms, marched boldly ahead, bouncing gently with the ramp, and at last stepped in triumph on to the curved seat of the stool.

"Hooray," said Max, very gently.

"Hooray!" echoed the Twelves from below. One by one the three other nameless soldiers stepped on to the gangway. Max piped them all aboard the stool with his song, until all four stood aloft, facing the rest on the floor. Last went the patriarch, and though one hundred and forty, he showed the same uprightness and agility as he had shown going downstairs. He settled himself cross-legged, in a patriarchal way, in front of the four others.

Butter held up his hands for silence.

"Now that the four kings, Sneaky, Wellington, Parry and Ross, are enthroned," he said, "you may begin the march past, and the triumphal entry of Stumps."

"Sneaky is not a very king-like name," Max could not help thinking. "I wonder if the lively fellow is Sneaky? It is just the kind of name I would give a soldier, and perhaps he became a king later."

Monkey scuttled over to beat the Ashanti drum which lay beside the stool and saw the flag. He let out a shrill yelp of glee, pounced on it and waved it. There was a slight argument as to who should bear the colours, and then Max saw Bravey grasp the flag by sheer elbowing power. Cheeky and Gravey fell in to support him, and the colour party set forth, the two middies behind.

They marched past the stool to the tiny sound of Monkey's tattoo, tum tiddle um tum, tum tiddle um tum, saluting as they passed the kings, who were solemnly saluting back. The patriarch did not salute, but held up both hands with palms facing, in a kind of blessing, to show that he was different.

Then the column went on, picked up Stumps and proceeding to the other side of the attic, swung round and began to march straight forward again to the stool.

And it was then that Max saw Jane. He had watched them round, of course, turning his head.

Jane's white face was peering at him from behind some furniture. Her blue eyes were as round as medals, she was pale to the lips, and her mouth was open.

The Four Kings of Ashanti

"Max!" she hissed, very softly. Max was horrified, much more because he thought Jane's presence would stop this wonderful parade than because he felt angry. He had no time to feel angry.

"Be quiet," he whispered in a tone of fierce command. "And keep still." Then he turned his attention to the Twelves. They had reached the ramp, halted, and presented Stumps. Stumps bowed, the soldiers cheered, Monkey beat a wild last tattoo, the four kings inclined their heads in a martial way and the patriarch nodded three times.

> *"Frederic Guelph Duke of York*
> *Frederic the First, King of the Twelves*
> *Afterwards made Frederic the Second*
> *Stumps, Stumps, here is Stumps*
> *Stumps, Stumps, back from the grave,"*

chanted the Twelves.

> *"Hail, Stumpy, hail, Tump head*
> *Never mind your bandy legs!"*

piped Bravey cheekily, on his own. Other soldiers quickly muffled him, and the patriarch pretended not to notice. Stumps merely smiled in a lofty way, secure in his kingship.

"Well," thought Max, "I'm glad they give him some honour, even if he did give up being king."

"Tell your tale, Stumps," said Butter.

And everyone stood at ease, including Monkey. Stumps stepped forward, and told his tale. Max had to lean down and listen hard to hear the words, for he had not heard Stumps speak before.

Stump's adventures were in every particular as he had imagined. He did not know what the S-bend below the sink was called, and he referred to it as a great, white creeper, in the crook of which he was safe. (This must be because he is so used to Africa, thought Max, where they have great twisty creepers.) He was even safe from a roaring animal that pursued things over the floor sucking everything into its maw. (This was Mrs. Hodgson's hoover.) When he had finished with his account of his climb to safety everyone clapped and cheered and broke ranks. It seemed the assembly was over.

"Maxy," said Jane. "I don't understand."

"Follow me out," he whispered, "and don't walk near them."

He tiptoed to the door. Jane followed. Max shut the Twelves in to finish their rejoicings and faced her on the landing.

Chapter 8

Alexander Sneaky

He looked at Jane with a kind of triumph. It was sad in a way that his secret was over, and now that he had time to think of it, it was mean of Jane to have hidden like that; but none the less, there was no question of Jane not believing, or laughing at him. Jane had seen it with her own eyes.

Jane was frightened and bewildered. She was looking at Max as if he were a person she had not known before.

"How do you do it?" she said huskily.

"At first," Max said, "it was when I beat the Ashanti drum. But this time, they did it on their own. They came downstairs too. That time I was in the kitchen and you all came back and Stumps got lost. He hid, you see. Jane, you've jolly well got to promise not to tell anyone else. Yet. After all, it was a bit beastly to hide like that."

"I know," Jane said, "I didn't mean to, I was just going to get the rest of my books from that trunk, and then I heard you coming and I thought it would be fun to hear your game. Because you wouldn't tell me. But I didn't know it was *this* kind of a secret," said Jane.

The colour had come back into her cheeks. Max took these tiny, lively creatures for granted. He did not seem frightened by their doings, so she need not. The strangeness of the little soldiers began to be overcome in her mind by the same excitement and delight as Max felt.

"Max. I'm sorry I hid," she went on. "But it's *marvellous!*"

Max nodded. He was appeased because Jane was so impressed.

"You can be a Genii too, if you like," he said generously, "and watch over them."

"What's a Genii? Like the Arabian Nights?"

"Sort of. I'm one. I look after them and they consult me. At least, Butter does."

"Is Butter the most important?"

"His real name's Butter Crashey. He's the patriarch, a hundred and forty. And he's the oracle for them, he comes to ask me things."

"How did you think of 'Butter Crashey'?"

"I didn't *think* of it, he told me," Max said, with scorn. "They know their names. And their ages. And they remember all about an expedition to Africa and a kingdom they had there. They tell me. What I think," explained Max, as he and Jane sat on the top stair, "is this, that the boys who had them before, and who were their Genii, made all this up."

"I see. What boys?"

"Well, some family must have had them. Over a hundred years ago, like Daddy said. And Butter says there were four. Four Genii. Or it may have been some girls, too," he said kindly. "So I expect you could be a Genii. If you wanted."

"I do," said Jane. "They're *sweet*," she said.

"You mustn't call them sweet," Max replied, "soldiers wouldn't like it. And they don't like me helping them too much, either. They have to do things their own way. Look, Jane, promise. You won't tell anyone. Yet."

Jane put her palm on Max's.

"I absolutely swear," she said.

"I'm going back, to ask B. Crashey about those other three kings. I didn't know there were four kings, till today."

"Can I come?" Jane pleaded.

"Not this time. I'll ask him about your being a Genii, shall I? You see, they're not used to you yet."

"All right," she said. "I'll wait here."

But Max was gone for a long time, and then the telephone bell rang, and Jane's mother called her. So, casting a longing glance at the closed attic door, she went down. Max had gone back into the attic, sat on the stool which was now deserted, and picked up Butter Crashey. The rest had moved the ramp from the stool to the Ashanti canoe, and with whoops of delight were climbing aboard it.

"I enjoyed the parade," began Max.

Butter Crashey seemed pleased, and his wise, wrinkled, patriarchal face creased into an endearing smile. It was the first time Max had noticed his smile.

"We knew that you would be present, oh protector of Stumps," he said.

"Butter Crashey, tell me about the other three kings. I know about Arthur Wellesley, Duke of Wellington, scourge of Napoleon," Max said, thinking this sounded very grand. "But why were there four kings?"

"We divided our kingdom amongst the Ashanti, into four parts," the patriarch explained. "Therefore there were four kings."

"Oh, I see," Max said, and he added eagerly: "Were there four kings because there were four Genii?" He had just thought of this.

Butter Crashey nodded wisely.

"No doubt," he said, "that was why. One to protect each king and each country."

"Of course," Max agreed. "I suppose the Genii chose the kings?"

"It is lost in the ancient days of the Young Men. But our legends say that the four Genii seized upon four chosen warriors, promised to protect them, and told them that they should one day all be kings."

"I'd choose Stumps," thought Max.

"Do the legends say," he asked, "what the names of the Genii were?" If he knows this, thought Max, I shall find out about this boy or boys who had them, so long ago.

Butter looked quite shocked.

"We have all known the names of the Genii," he protested, "since time out of mind."

"Can you tell me what they were?" Max asked boldly.

"The chief Genius was Brannii, the others were Tallii, Emmii and Annii." Max sighed. They were very made-up names, but of course he should have expected this.

"Did they live here, in this very place?" he asked.

"Who can say where the Genii live? They are not confined to houses but often reside in the desert or the hills or the strange places of the clouds," Butter said solemnly. "All the same," he added in a more practical tone, "their abode was not very far from here."

"And do you know, Butter Crashey," Max asked next, "which Genii chose which soldier?"

"Who should know but I?" said the patriarch. "It was after the building of our first town in Africa. I had gone into the desert to seek out the Genii. While the rest were sitting together in the common hall, the air suddenly darkened, the hall shook and streams of fire continually flashed through the room, followed by long and loud peals of thunder. . . . You may read it in *The History of the Young Men*," he said. Max was disappointed, for he was afraid that the patriarch had finished speaking and he did not know where to find *The History of the Young Men*, even if there really were such a book.

Alexander Sneaky

"What happened next?" he said eagerly.

"A dreadful Monster entered the room with me in his hand. He placed me down, gently (for although the Genii are terrible to us in power, we have learnt to know they are kindly disposed), and said in a loud voice. . . ." Butter paused.

"Yes?" Max whispered.

" 'I am the chief Genius Brannii, with me there are three others; she, Wellesley, who protects you is named Tallii, she who protects Parry is named Emmii, she who protects Ross is called Annii. . . . We are the guardians of this land, we are the guardians of you all. Revere this man Crashey, he is entrusted with secrets which you can never know.' " At this point Crashey winked very solemnly, yet Max thought he could detect a twinkle in his black mouse-like eyes. "Then he spread out his dragon wings and flew away," said the patriarch.

"So," said Max, who had been listening intently, "there was one boy Genius and three girl Genii?"

"That is so," Butter said.

One boy, Max thought, and three sisters.

"And now in these degenerate days," the patriarch added rather sadly, "we are reduced to one Genius only, yourself, oh Maxii. How are the mighty fallen," he added, sniffing.

Max liked Maxii, it sounded much more like a Genius.

"A new Genius has come," he explained, "whose name is Janeii."

Butter looked very pleased, and nodded.

"Come, that's better," he said dropping his oracle's manner, "we shall be more protected, and such accidents as befell Stumps lately may be prevented."

"Butter Crashey," asked Max next, "which soldier did the Chief Genius protect? Was it Sneaky, the very lively one? Do you know, right at the beginning, I saw him make you alive—I mean to say——" Max stopped, confused—"it looked as if he woke you all up."

"No wonder," Butter said, not at all put out. "Alexander Sneaky it is, and he was the first favourite of the Chief Genius Brannii, the red-headed. He is certainly lively, though he has

57

moods, and strikes attitudes. He is ingenious, artful, deceitful but courageous," explained the patriarch. "No wonder he woke us up. Did we not live under the protection of the Chief Genius Brannii? And Sneaky is his man."

"Of course. I see," Max answered. And he thought to himself that the Chief Genius must have started the game and kept it going, and perhaps the soldiers were really his, as he was the boy.

"And Parry?" Max said. "What's he like?"

"There he is, climbing the prow of that ship now, by a secret way," said Butter, pointing. Parry had scorned the ramp, and scrambling over some books and papers was about to drop down over the bows and take the rest by surprise.

"He is fifteen, and a brave sailor-like young man, but a little too fond of subterfuge. . . ." Butter said.

What sneaks these kings seem to be, thought Max, but it is better than being all the same and dull old heroes.

"How are the mighty fallen!" said Butter again, as Tracky shot up from the canoe and hit Parry smartly down to the ground again with a piece of balsa. Max laughed, and even the patriarch was seen to smile.

"And Ross, what's Ross doing?" Max asked.

"There he is, standing on the gunwale. Sixteen years, frank, open, honest and of a bravery when in battle sometimes approaching to madness. Though I admit he is a queer looking thing to look at, he was the protected of the Genius Annii."

One sister, thought Max, was called Anne.

"Maxy, Maxy!" called his mother, and it sounded as if her feet were upon the very stair of the attic.

"Help!" Max gasped. And he put down the patriarch in the boat, and dashed from the room with a clatter and a bang.

And that, he thought, as he ran to the stairs, is what they call thunder.

Chapter 9

Mr. Rochester

The telephone bell had been Mrs. Rochester (as Jane now called her) asking them to tea. Their mother never accepted invitations for them without making sure that her children had not arranged anything else and, even more important, that they wanted to go. She had asked Jane, and now she asked Max.

He met her on the first landing, and they proceeded together down to Jane.

"Do *you* want to go, Janey?" asked Max. He was hoping she would say she did not, because he had looked forward to their first time together with the Young Men. On the other hand, he had liked Mr. Howson.

Jane knew what Max was thinking, but all the same she wanted to go.

"Yes, I do," she said.

"What, just because you think he's like that old Mr. Rochester?" Max said rather grumpily. Jane grinned.

"Well, you liked him," she said, "you told me so."

"He was interested in my soldiers," Max explained.

"Yes, he's a great antiquarian," said Mrs. Morley, "and sometime you must show them to him."

"What's a great antiquarium?" Max asked, in tones of disgust. Max often sounded disgusted when he did not understand.

"A person who loves and knows about old things," she explained.

"*I* thought it was to do with fishes," said Max, unbelievingly.

"That's an aquarium," said his mother. Max looked sideways at Jane.

"First, he's an old brontyfan with a great long neck," he said, "and then he's an antiquarium with fishes swimming about inside him," he added, trying to make Jane laugh, and succeeding. Jane was excited anyway, and she now began to giggle until Max joined in, and they both laughed until Mrs. Morley had to laugh too; and they were pushing each other about in the hall, with red faces, when in strode Philip.

"What's the joke," he said, "you silly little things?"

"Phil," Jane gasped, "do you want to go to tea with Mr. and Mrs. Rochester?"

"No," said Philip at once. "Thanks," he added.

"Oh, Philip," said his mother. "I've got to ring back. What can I say? Besides, you won't see much of them, I don't suppose, it's to get to know their family. There's a boy just a little younger than you—and you'll never guess, there are triplets, girls."

The three Morleys seemed stunned by this information. They stared at their mother.

"*That's* not a bit like Mr. Rochester," Jane said, perfectly solemn, and in an outraged tone.

"Why didn't you *tell* us?" said Max, who thought that triplets were so unusual as to be worth going to see.

"I haven't had the chance yet, with you two being so silly."

"Anyway," Philip put in gloomily, "what difference does triplets make? How old?"

"About Jane's age."

"It'll be Jane multiplied by three," said her brother, making a face at her. "One's enough."

"Let's go," said Jane.

"Shall we, Maxy? We'll be outnumbered, by one," Philip said.

"All right," said Max, liking to find himself bracketed with Philip. "Where have you been?"

Mrs. Morley went to the telephone, with a feeling of relief.

"All over the place," Phil said. "The heather's gorgeous, and I've been through Haworth, where all these old Brontë fans go, and seen the parsonage, where the Brontës lived."

"Did you go in?" said Jane.

"No, I shall wait till Mummy takes us, then she'll pay," he said softly, winking at his sister.

Philip was inclined to be careful with his money.

Mrs. Morley was right: they did not at first see much of Mr. and Mrs. Howson, for they were greeted in the vicarage drive by the young Howsons and at once taken on a tour of both the house and the garden, a proceeding which seems to be necessary before two families get to know each other. Christopher Howson was tall and pale like his father and he and Philip rushed off, talking hard, towards a shrubbery.

"Come on," he yelled.

The three girls, who were alike and not alike, enclosed Jane and began to ask at once if she were coming to their school.

Max trailed along behind, rather forlorn, beginning to wish he had not come. He would rather have been with the Twelves. There was Jane, the new Genii, and she had utterly forgotten.

"Max, keep with us," called Philip, "we want you, against this monstrous regiment of women."

Max did not entirely understand this, but he knew it meant, for the moment, boys against girls, and anyway it made all the difference to his feelings. He tore past the girls, making a noise like a train whistle, and came up with Philip and Christopher in the shrubbery. They were shown the best trees to climb, and the view from the top. They inspected a potting shed, a grotto, and a private loose brick, where the girls posted secret letters. Christopher's tour included the fruit trees, where Max stole an apple, and the cabbages, and the lawn and the chickens.

Then they made for the house and entered it like a mountain torrent. By this time everybody knew everybody, nobody was shy, and their seven voices, all talking at once and shouting to be heard, filled the vicarage with a noise like a market day. Each door they came to was rushed at by a Howson and the room introduced as if it were a person. More often than not Christopher and one or other of his sisters had a fight at the door knob. The doors slammed or swung behind them as they impatiently went on to the next.

Jane had a feeling that this was not a very polite way of going out to tea, but there was no doubt that it left no room for shyness. She was behind the rest, who had just charged upstairs. Max was far too excited, stamping. There was a door next to the drawing-room, which nobody had opened. Perhaps it could not hurt to peep inside. She turned the handle gently, and looked in.

Over by the window stood the tall, black, sombre figure of the parson, gazing out at the jagged cedar tree and lost, it was certain, in his own tragic thoughts.

"Oh, Mr. Rochester, sorry," gasped Jane.

For he had turned round and was looking at her without seeing her, it seemed, his eyes dark in his pale face. At least, this is what Jane thought.

"Come in, come in, Jane," he said, and he laughed. "*What* did you call me?" Jane walked into the room very gently and gracefully, as she always did, and not knowing quite what to say. She looked at her feet and then up at Mr. Howson.

"Mr. Rochester," she said very softly. "We call you Mr. Rochester at home, because I think you're like him, and I'm sorry, I got muddled up."

"And do you know who I think you're like," he said, "I think you're like Jane Eyre."

Jane looked pleased and smiled.

"Have you just been reading it?" he asked.

"Yes, I love it, I love Mr. Rochester, I'm going to begin reading it again."

"Most girls like Mr. Rochester," he said. "I suppose because he's so mysterious?"

Jane nodded. She did not know why she liked him, but this might be one reason. Her face was flushed with racing round the garden, and glowing with her ideas about Mr. Rochester. And Mr. Howson thought to himself that Jane would grow up soon into a beautiful girl and have to marry a quite ordinary man, like himself, like any man, and not at all like the amazing Mr. Rochester. Whereupon he prayed to God there and then to send her a good, true one who should value the flame inside her and not dim it. He laughed again, as a clatter of feet sounded overhead.

"Aren't we making a noise," Jane said. "Will Mrs. Howson mind? They're showing us the house."

"No, she won't mind. See you at tea, Jane," he said, waving, and she whirled round, soft as a feather, and skipped out.

Mr. Rochester

And at tea, Max was quite talkative. It must have been the race round the garden, and the clatter through the attics, and the sliding down the banisters; or perhaps the game of clock golf which they had played afterwards. Whatever it was he felt entirely at home and very friendly towards Mr. Howson, by whom he was sitting.

"I found the lost soldier," he said.

"Oh, did you, Max, I'm glad of that. Now tell me again, where did you find these soldiers?"

Max told the tale, and he told it well, describing how he had stepped on the squeaky, uneven board. By the time he had finished, everybody was listening. "And inside this old roll of rag, were all the soldiers," he said, "one by one."

"And Max has done nothing but fug in the attic playing with them ever since," said Philip, "and Mummy thinks it's unhealthy."

"I can remember being crazed with soldiers," said Christopher, as if this were years and years ago.

"And what do you do with them?" asked Mrs. Howson.

"Oh, Mummy! You set them all out and parade them and kill them off in battles and make them alive again and bomb them, and take them on forced marches, and all that."

"And you give them all names," said Philip. "Field Marshal So and So and Major-General What's-It."

Max was staring at Jane with bright mischievous grey eyes: and Jane was smiling back with wide, secretive blue ones. She had forgotten all about Mr. Rochester and remembered the wonderful secret again. Max laughed out of sheer pleasure at these people not knowing. Not knowing that he did not have to do things, that Butter and the Duke and the rest, especially Stumps, did things on their own.

"But Maxy's names are the dottiest you ever heard," Philip went on. "Butter, for instance."

"Butter!" shrieked one of the triplets. "Why?"

"For one reason," Max said quickly, "he fell in the butter."

"You know, Max," said Mr. Howson, "you remind me to tell you about the Brontë family, who lived at Haworth near here. When they were small, they had soldiers. And they had such vivid

63

imaginations, that they made up the most exciting adventures for their soldiers to have."

"Did they?" Max said. "How do you know?"

"We know because they were born writers and wrote it down. Even when they were quite young. And it went on for years and years. There are books and books of it: exercise books you know, and some so tiny, you can hardly see the writing. I think Branwell and Charlotte wrote the most, but they all played these games. Jane knows about Charlotte, she's been reading *Jane Eyre*, she tells me. I can't remember the names of all the stories, but I know one was called *The History of the Young Men*."

Max stopped chewing and gazed at Mr. Howson in astonishment, his mouth open.

"Max, do swallow your mouthful," said Philip, nudging him.

"And they gave all theirs names, too, of course. Some were after famous real people, and some were just fun, like yours. In fact I'm not sure one of theirs wasn't Butter. Butter something. And I expect that's what reminded me. I must look it up again."

Max closed his mouth, and gazed at his plate, and took another piece of bread and butter, and said absolutely nothing. He dared not look at Jane. He felt himself going red. And then he felt himself feeling quite faint and fluttery like he did when he knew he had done something wrong and was about to be found out and blamed. Mr. Howson thought that he had bored Max, by talking of things he did not know about, and Mrs. Howson thought that there was a sudden silence and she had better fill it. And Philip thought Max was behaving very oddly, not to say rudely; and the Howson family thought their father needed stopping when he began to talk about the Brontës. So they all started suddenly to say things together, and then everyone laughed, and tried again, and the awkward moment passed. Max's wooden soldiers were forgotten, by everyone except Max and Jane.

Chapter 10

The Four Genii

"Janey, come up to the attic," Max whispered, as they put the bicycles away. Philip had already gone off towards the farmyard.

Jane nodded eagerly at once, and Max felt relieved. She had not forgotten, she was still a faithful Genii or Genius. He was not sure which.

"Yes," she said.

They pelted up the stairs without talking, and as Mrs. Morley came out of the kitchen to ask them if they had enjoyed themselves she thought: Ah, Jane's in Max's game now, evidently. And she wondered what it was that absorbed them so.

"Wasn't it funny about the Brontës having soldiers," Jane said softly as they approached the attic door.

"*Funny*," said Max, in a tone heavy with excitement and meaning. "Janey, do you realize, that thing he said they wrote, called *The History of the Young Men*, is what Butter talked about this morning?"

Jane stared at Max.

"You didn't tell me."

"I haven't had a chance yet, have I?"

"Is that why you went red and shut up?"

"Yes, did I? Well, it gave me a shock. And then, one being called Butter Something! He said so, 'Butter Something', and that's what had reminded him!"

"Yes, he did. Max, what do you think it is? Do you think. . . ?"

Max interrupted her.

"How many of these old Brontës were there?"

"Four, I think."

The Four Genii

"There you are. Butter says there were four Genii! Was there a boy and three girls?"

"I believe so, I'm not sure, I know about Charlotte most."

"Well, who can we ask? Do you know their names, Jane?"

"Only Charlotte. But, Maxy, if you think these are their soldiers, why are they *here*? They ought to be at Haworth, where they lived, not in an attic here."

"I can't help where they ought to be," Max said, excited, and rather cross because it all seemed strange and he did not understand it, "the thing is, *are* they the ones? Can you ask Mummy their names, these Brontës's names, without letting on *why*, Jane?"

"Why do you want to know their names?" she argued, feeling cross too.

"Because Butter told me the names of the four Genii," Max almost shouted. "I want to know if they fit in, you see. They're made up ones, the Genii, but they're sure to be from their real names." This conversation had been carried out, at first in secret whispers, outside the attic door. Their impatience, however, had made their voices grow louder and louder. Max suddenly realized this.

"Shush!" he said.

"Well, it's you to shush," retorted Jane with reason. "Wait here, don't go in without me, and I'll go and ask Mummy."

Max promised to wait. But he could not resist kneeling down and looking through the keyhole.

There was not a soldier to be seen. The space before the Ashanti stool was empty. However, he could not survey the whole attic from the keyhole, and he had promised not to go in.

Jane returned, to find him kneeling before the door. She was breathless, and as she knelt too, she giggled.

"This is how I saw you when you first started it, and you had that gob-stopper."

"I *didn't* start it," Max protested. "They've gone," he added. "What are the names?"

"What do you mean, GONE?" Jane said, shocked, pushing him aside and putting her blue eye to the keyhole. "Max!"

The Four Genii

"Well, they walk about. We'll go in soon. What are the four names?"

Jane raised her head.

"Charlotte, Branwell, Emily and Anne," she said. "In that order. There were two older ones that died."

Max looked at her, remembering.

"Well, the Genii were called Brannii, Tallii, Emmii, and Annii," he said slowly.

They both squatted back, on their heels.

"The only one that isn't right is Tallii," said Jane.

"Brannii was the chief Genius. That's the boy, Branwell, isn't it?"

"Yes. He was Patrick Branwell, but as their father was Patrick too he was called Branwell, Mummy said."

"Was she suspicious?"

"No, she just said she supposed Mr. Rochester had got us interested and I said yes, I was as vague as anything."

"Good. I'd already guessed Anne. Emmii is Emily. So, Tallii must be your Charlotte one."

"It ought to be Charlii."

"Well, I expect she thought that was too like a boy."

"Yes."

"You see, Butter called me Maxii, and then I called you Janeii."

"All to go with Genii," added Jane.

"Let's go in and I'll say you're here."

"Yes," Jane said, very excited. "Max, can I hold one, like you do?"

"I think you might hold Butter, he's the one who's used to speaking to the Genii. We'll see what happens."

They went in, and gazed all round the attic, in each corner. No Young Men.

"Perhaps they're behind something," Max whispered.

"Where do you keep them, in that shoe box?"

"Yes, but they wouldn't put themselves away."

"They could. Oh, Max——" she clutched his arm—"they're in the boat!"

They were. Only the heads and shoulders of the Twelves

showed, above the sides of the carved canoe. What is more, their heads were drooped upon their hands, and their hands were clutching balsa wood oars, which rested on their little knees and over the side of the canoe. They were asleep, it seemed.

"Worn out, with rowing," whispered Max. Butter sat in the bows, his head bent forward on his chest; Crackey sat in the stern, or rather leaned back, sleeping comfortably. Between them sat the rest, in two rows of five, holding their oars, of different lengths, and looking like galley slaves.

Max and Jane kneeled down to look at them.

"Have they gone back to being wooden?" Jane asked.

Max looked fixedly at Butter. As he looked, he could make out, perhaps, the slightest rise and fall of his breathing. He was not sure.

Then he looked at Crackey's face, the only face that showed, and realized that he had known it was Crackey, which meant his face was not wooden and blurred but lively and detailed. "No. They're just asleep," he said.

And at this moment, the patriarch awoke, stretched his arms, yawned, rubbed his eyes, and said in a brisk voice: "Ready all."

"Oh, his darling yawn," said Jane.

"Jane, don't treat him like a toy, or a baby animal, will you?" warned Max. He felt that this would be wrong and insulting. "He's a small, alive person," he explained, "and full of years and wisdom, he says so."

"Yes, I see," she said meekly.

All the rest sat up at his words, balanced their oars as best they could without rowlocks, many finding them too heavy, and began to row, rather wildly, as Butter directed.

"One, two; one, two; one, two," said the patriarch briskly.

"Mind your elbows, Cheeky," growled Gravey.

"Old sourpuss," retorted the bold Cheeky.

"I should be obliged if His present Majesty could keep his knees out of my back," requested Stumps of the Duke of Wellington.

"Impossible to achieve," drawled the Duke, "since you push your back into my knees."

" 'Brave Benbow lost his legs, by chain-shot, by chain-sho-o-ot,' " yelled Crackey from the stern, to the time of the rowing.

"Move over, Ross," snarled Parry.

"How can I, the boat's curved, and throws you into the middle like a feather bed," said Ross, crossly. With all this argument, the rowing became wilder and wilder. Max and Jane watched, half-smiling and half-alarmed, as the cries and arguments of the Twelves grew loud. Sneaky found it impossible to row properly sitting down, so he leapt up and began using his piece of wood like a punt pole over the side, to the peril of Tracky, who sat in his way.

"That's Sneaky," whispered Max, "and he was the favourite of the chief Genius Brannii. Butter told me so. He's one of the kings, do you remember?"

"He would be," said Jane.

"We're not getting far, anyway," said Monkey, "without any water."

"You look as if you're waving a flag, not rowing a boat," said Cheeky.

Monkey raised his oar, which was certainly short, and brought it down crack on Cheeky's head. Cheeky returned the blow, but his oar glanced off and hit Gravey. Gravey howled, stood up, and began hitting everyone at random, even while still wearing an expression of the utmost melancholy. Sneaky was quick to join him.

At once, there was pandemonium in the Ashanti canoe, as all the rowers jumped up.

"Help," said Jane, "how do you stop a quarrel?"

"I've never had to, Butter usually does," whispered Max.

Butter was standing up with raised arms, calling, "Easy all," but nobody took much notice. By now they were whacking and punching with great abandon, and the canoe was rocking a little on the attic floor.

Max swooped upon Butter and lifted him high.

"Command silence, oh Patriarch," he suggested. The patriarch blinked, but finding himself in a position of such advantage, he said loudly, "Pray silence!" And as they heard this voice, apparently from the courts of heaven, the Twelves ceased their fight, sat down and rubbed their bruises.

"Butter Crashey," said Max solemnly, "the Genii Janeii is present," and he could hardly forbear to laugh, for Genii Janeii sounded so unexpectedly funny.

The patriarch's wise, wrinkled face took on a look of satisfaction. Jane was watching intently, smiling. Max held Butter towards her, signing to her to take him.

Jane put her finger and thumb round his body, and felt the taut, thrilling wriggle of life. She could not help a slight shiver.

"Welcome, oh Genii, on behalf of the Young Men," the patriarch said, and he bowed his top half in her hand, and looked up smiling. Jane smiled back. His eyes were as bright and beady as a mouse's. She was enchanted.

"I am glad to be here, oh Patriarch," she replied with natural grace, having noted the way Max addressed him.

From the boat there came the sound of a thin cheer. All malice and sulks seemed to be over.

"They welcome you," said Butter Crashey, nodding.

"Put him back in the boat, Jane," Max whispered, as they heard their mother ring the gong for supper. Jane did so, and as they

70

crept from the attic, they heard the Young Men's voices rise into a sea song.

"We'll rant and we'll roar," they shrilled, "all o'er the wild ocean. . . ."

"Max, the *feel* of him," Jane said, as they ran downstairs.

"I know. You can always tell when they freeze, they feel wooden again."

"Yes, I see. I love the way they sing."

"Now listen to this," said Mr. Morley, when the plates were served. And he reached behind him and brought forward the local paper. "Just listen. Here we are, letters to the Editor. It's from America." And he began to read:

Sir,

Is it too much to hope that somewhere, lurking unrecognized in some attic of farm-house or vicarage, or perhaps treasured but unknown amongst the objects in the drawing-room cabinet, there may survive some of the original wooden soldiers, Napoleonic in outfit and design, which—nay I would rather say, who—inspired the children of Haworth with their earliest, fertile imaginings?

Where are the noble Twelves, the Young Men, beloved of Branwell and his sisters, who, with their imaginary descendants, peopled all the early stories of this brilliant family? Could we but find them, would it not add much to our understanding of the thwarted genius of Branwell to study these little figures? I am ready to purchase them for the price of £5,000 sterling, or to reward suitably anyone leading me to the discovery of any of them.

I remain, sir,
Your obedient servant,
SENECA D. BREWER (Prof.).

The University,
  etc.

"Now, isn't that just going too far, I ask you, understanding the thwarted genius of Branwell Brontë by examining his wooden soldiers! Richest thing I've read in years. And as if they'd still be extant, made of *wood*, you know."

The family had sat silent, except for Philip, who had laughed at the professor's name. Max and Jane gazed at each other, and then looked quickly away. Mrs. Morley spoke. "But, Rod, Maxy's are wooden, and they have survived!" she said. "They're nearly as old, I suppose!"

"I know, I thought of Maxy's, it seemed a strange coincidence. But his were carefully wrapped up and put away, don't you see." And he began to eat his supper, with appetite. "If the Brontës's had been carefully put away they'd have been found, at Haworth, by now!"

"Five thousand pounds!" whistled Philip.

"Scholarship gone mad," said Mr. Morley. "As if a wooden soldier, or even a set of wooden soldiers, could tell you anything!"

"But it's an entertaining idea," said Mrs. Morley.

"What d'you wager me, half the families in Yorkshire will suddenly find wooden soldiers in their attics?" he said.

Max felt as if his food were choking him; Jane took frequent and large gulps of water. Her cheeks were burning. Max was afraid somebody would notice.

Chapter 11

The History
of the Young Men

When his mother came upstairs to tuck Max in, she was carrying a large book, which looked very learned. Max and Jane had had a hurried and rather frightened discussion in the bathroom. Max had said it was as good as proved whose the soldiers were. Jane had asked what would happen if this old professor found the right soldiers; would he take them to America? Because if so they must be more careful than ever to be secret and to protect them; for they both agreed that Butter Crashey and the rest would be stunned and terrified to be taken to America.

Max was lying in bed, wondering what was likely to happen next, following this strange turn of events. What worried him most was the extreme liveliness and activity of the Twelves. Anyone might see them at any minute, should he go into the attic. Their boldness had increased the more he had got to know them, and their habit of freezing from fear had grown less and less. With this letter in the paper, his father and Philip and Mr. Howson, and all the Howson family were likely to take an interest in them.

"Maxy! Do listen," said Mrs. Morley, sitting on the bed, "I thought you'd be so interested, so I dug this out to read to you. It's a story Branwell Brontë wrote about his wooden soldiers, and it's called *The History of the Young Men*. He was only twelve when he wrote it."

"Where'd you get it? Mr. Howson told us about it," said Max, trying to hide his excitement. "Call Janey, too."

"Janey! Come and hear this." Jane came pattering in. "I remembered I'd got this volume of some of the stories the Brontës wrote when they were children. Look, Max, here's the list of the soldiers! *Look* at their names! One is Butter Crashey, isn't that funny, like your Butter!" Her finger ran down the list of soldiers. "And it gives their ages. There's even one called Stumps! Jane, he's hit on two of their names," she said, delighted. "Isn't he clever? Or had you heard about them at school?"

Max had twisted round in bed, and was reading the list, pointing at it. There they all were. Butter Crashey, captain, 140: and all the others in order as he had got to know them. It was extraordinary. Max could hardly believe his eyes, but he remained quite cool. It was, in a way, no more than he had expected. He grinned at his mother. "You see, I'm as brilliant as these Brontës," he said, giggling. "Actually, Stumps has got stumpy legs, and Butter fell in the butter." Both these facts were quite true.

"Mummy," Jane said, "if this professor finds them, will he take them to America?"

"Oh yes, sure to. But there'll be an awful fuss from Haworth if he does. I'm afraid he's not likely to find them, however, because look what Branwell says, I've been reading it, where is it? Here we are. . . . First he describes all his earlier sets of soldiers, and then he says. . . . "on June the 5th A.D. 1826 Papa procured me from Leeds another set (these were the 12s) which I kept for 2 years, though 2 or 3 of them are in being at the time of my writing this (Dec 15 A.D. 1830)." And then he goes on about some later sets. He was eight when he had them, Maxy, your age. And he says by 1830 only 2 or 3 were left."

But Max and Jane, who were quite silent for a minute, knew better.

"Well," explained Max, for some explanation he knew there must be, "you see, *he* only had two or three, but that doesn't mean the others weren't somewhere. He could have just lost them, around the place, and someone else could have picked them up and kept them."

"Yes," said Jane eagerly, "one of the girls easily could, you know, Mummy. Girls are much carefuller than boys, they keep things longer too, and they sort of can't bear to throw things away. I can't bear to throw away some of my tiny things even though I

74

don't play with them any longer!" Jane was speaking very earnestly. "It's because girls love things longer."

Mrs. Morley wondered what Max would say to this.

"I think that's true, Janey. What do you think, Max?"

"I think," Max said solemnly, "they may love them for longer, I don't know, but they couldn't love them more. They absolutely couldn't love them more. Than I love the old soldiers now, say."

"So boys love things more strongly while they love them, and girls love them for longer, is that it? I think you may be about right. Anyway, you must settle down, Max. It'll be very funny to see if anyone claims to find the Brontës's soldiers and gets the £5,000."

"It's rather exciting, really, isn't it," said Jane, watching her mother closely.

"Well, it could be if there were any way of knowing they were really the ones. But, you see, wooden soldiers are all much alike. If anyone's got a set of about the right time, he could easily *say* they were the ones. But there's no proving it."

"That's what Daddy meant then?" Jane said.

"Yes. He thinks someone will offer any old set to get the £5,000," and she laughed, kissing Max. "I'll leave the book in case you want to read it in the morning. Good night, Maxy. Hurry up, Jane, it's late."

"Yes, I just want to tell Max something."

When their mother had gone, Jane said quickly:

"Isn't it hard *not* to tell her? Shall we?"

"Not yet, no. We may have to, though," Max replied.

Max lay awake a long time, thinking of his soldiers. First he thought how strange it was that his mother had said wooden soldiers were all much alike, and how astonished and delighted she would be if she could see their faces go different and lively instead of blurred and wooden. He knew she would be delighted, he could imagine her face. She had often said to him how amazing it was that God had made everybody absolutely different from every other body. Well, it was the same with the soldiers. Whoever had carved them, had made them different, with great care, and it was his mother who had pointed this out. And then the four Genii, by imagining all these things, had added to it, had made them into real people. He sat up and drew back the curtain and dragged the heavy book up to the window. He looked at the page his mother had left open, and his eye fell on one sentence.

". . . what is contained in this History is a statement of what myself, Charlotte, Emily and Anne really pretended did happen among the 'Young Men' (that being the name we gave them) during the period of nearly 6 years. . . ."

Max flopped back, leaving the book on the sill.

And the Genii imagined them all so real, he thought to himself, that the Young Men still remember, they are still alive. Could this be what it was? And then he fell to thinking of them in turn, and which he loved best. He had told Jane and his mother that nobody could love anything more than he loved the Twelves. Now. And this was true. He wondered if this was another reason why they were so lively, because he loved them and they trusted him. Nobody could help loving Butter Crashey. Max thought how Branwell and his sisters had each had a special one they loved, and made kings. And no wonder King Sneaky, Branwell's soldier, was the first to wake up with the drum, the first to make the others alive! No wonder. It was Branwell's game, and Sneaky was his man, as Butter had said. It all fitted in. He realized that his own special one was Stumps. It was because he had lost him and found him again and guarded him and brought him back to the attic when he had so bravely climbed the creeper. He had had more to do with Stumps than anyone so far. He wondered whose Jane's was, or would be.

But it was a mystery as to how they had reached this attic, all together, and none lost, when Branwell said only two or three were left. Perhaps it was what Jane suggested, one of the girls had been careful. Max suddenly felt a strange urge to go and ask Butter this at once. For surely Butter would know?

He scrambled out of bed and tiptoed to the door. Jane had long since settled down. His mother and father and Philip must be still downstairs, though Philip would soon be coming up. It was safe. He crept up the attic stairs, and then saw with a shock that the door was open and the light was on.

Philip was kneeling on the floor by the canoe, picking up the

Twelves one by one, turning them over, looking at them, as if they were what he thought they were, simply pieces of wood.

Max had a very quick temper. He now felt a huge hot wave of rage coming up in his throat from his heart, ready to drown him.

"Put my soldiers down, they're not yours, I haven't said you can touch them," he said in a hoarse, choking voice. "Put them down," he screamed, with his fists clenched, and his teeth grinding together, as Philip turned round in amazement. "Put them down. You'll hurt them, you'll break them, who said you could touch them?"

"All right, all right, I'm only *looking* at them, I shan't hurt them. It's jolly interesting, after what that old professor says. Did you arrange them all, with their oars balanced, in the canoe? Anyway, who said you could borrow my balsa?" Philip added, seizing on this advantage. And he collected Butter, and Stumps, and Sneaky and Cheeky and Gravey from his knee, and tossed them, head first, higgledy-piggledy, back into the boat, where they lay sprawled with all the others, who had evidently been similarly treated. The oars were fallen in all directions.

The thing in Max's heart burst.

"You're not to throw them about!" he screamed.

He dived at Philip, who was barely up from the ground, he beat him with his knuckles, he kicked him, he bit him, he scratched him. But Philip was much older and much stronger, he was fourteen. He soon mastered the furious Max, trying hard to keep his own temper.

"Paddy, paddy," he breathed, losing it, as Max kicked. And he flung Max off on to the attic floor, hard, and went out slamming the door.

"You've hurt them, you've killed them," Max sobbed and he lay on the floor a long time, wanting to kill Philip, and crying because he could not stop crying. It was all spoilt, they would be frozen again, they might even be broken. He hardly dared to look.

He sat up at last, feeling weak and wretched as anyone does who has lost his temper, and his eyes were so swollen he could hardly see through them. He rubbed them. He heard a familiar whispery, whisking noise. He peered anxiously at the canoe.

The Twelves were sitting, tidily and neatly, along the bottom, engaged in earnest conversation. They were evidently discussing what had happened. They seemed very excited, and none was hurt. Sneaky was on his feet, waving his arms about as if he were talking to a public meeting.

Max put out his hand, and took Butter Crashey gently from the bows of the boat.

"Are you hurt, oh Patriarch?" he said, sniffing, but comforted to feel Butter's lizard body in his fingers.

"An immense monster seized upon us all in turn," he said, "and after turning us round as if we were sacks of coals, or potatoes, tossed us without ceremony through the air; we, not recognizing him, remained frozen."

"I know, I saw, I was afraid you were hurt," Max whispered.

"Hurt?" questioned Butter, with dignity. "We who have been through such perils? Sailing in the *Invincible* (a deal better than this boat we are reduced to), conquering the Ashanti, carving out our kingdom, building our cities?"

Max smiled and nodded.

"Also," said the patriarch, "have you forgotten the secret process of being made alive? We, whom the four Genii constantly made alive, and protected? We, who were collected from the four corners where we were scattered in old age, and were banded together again, indestructible, the Twelves, the Young Men? Hurt?" he demanded, drawing himself proudly up in Max's hand and at the same time stumbling slightly in the rut between Maxy's fingers.

"Oh, Butter Crashey," said Max, careful not to smile, "of course not, I am sorry I insulted you." And then he remembered the question he had come to ask, and realized it was partly answered. "Who collected you from the four corners? One of the female Genii?"

"That I cannot say, for it is lost in the mists of antiquity," said the patriarch. And he shook his head.

Max put Butter gently back amongst the chattering Twelves, and went to bed, worn out with his feelings.

Chapter 12

Five Thousand Pounds

The book which contained the story of the Young Men had gone when Max woke up. He supposed his mother must have come in and taken it after he was asleep and forgotten to put it back.

In fact, Philip had taken it, after he had left Max crying in the attic. He was now sitting up in bed continuing to read it, and everything else in the volume which concerned the wooden soldiers the professor was looking for. He had studied Max's soldiers with a detailed and scientific interest such as he applied to his work at school. He had already noticed, in the shoe box where Max kept them, a few of the round stands that balanced them, and he had now found in the book Branwell's own description of what the soldiers looked like, including these round stands, which he referred to as their one shoe. "This shoe, for each man wore only one! was like a round flat cake with two holes in the middle into which his feet were inserted as in a stocks," Branwell had written. And at the bottom of the page in a footnote he had added, "the curious shoe was the little stand which each soldier had to keep him from falling". Philip also thought Branwell's description of what they wore tallied with Max's soldiers, ". . . a high black cap with several hieroglyphical figures on it . . .", but these, naturally, he thought, would be rubbed off by now. "Their coat or rather jacket was shaped after the manner of a sailor's and was in colour a light scarlet. They also wore light pantaloons of the same colour." There was not much colour left now, but they certainly had been scarlet. Now Philip, in his time, had been just as keen on soldiers, and he could not help a feeling of excitement that here might be

the very ones this famous Branwell had written about. He read
backwards and forwards in the book: he found Charlotte's description of how each girl seized a soldier from Branwell's new box,
named him and called him hers; he found the bit where Branwell
said that two or three (only) were still in being. But like Max, he
was not unduly worried by this. Someone else could have collected
and preserved what Branwell had lost or broken.

Now, if it could be proved they were the ones, was not Max good
for five thousand pounds? Philip was a practical boy, and he liked
money. He had been going to suggest to Maxy that he would help
him write the letter to the professor, describing his find, for a small
percentage to be paid when he had received his five thousand. But
Max had been in such a devilish temper that he could say nothing
then of this plan. And also he had an idea that Max was so be-
sotted with these soldiers he might not *want* to sell them. Why
otherwise had he flown into such a rage at his touching them? Of
course, Philip knew there was a kind of unwritten law in the family
about not playing with each other's things without asking. He supposed he should have asked, and he did not quite know why he had
not, except that Max was in bed and his curiosity overcame him.

When Philip came to the list of soldiers and re-read it carefully,
noticing Butter Crashey was one hundred and forty, he did think
it odd. Somehow Max could have heard the *name*, or of course
made it up in the way he said, when the soldier fell in the butter.
But that he should also be one hundred and forty. . . . Max must
have got hold of this book, perhaps, and read the list? Or someone
at school had told them about the Brontë soldiers? That was more
likely. The same reasons could account for "Stumps", whose
name he saw further down. Max had remembered some of the
names he had been told, and used them. But in that case, if he
knew about the Brontë soldiers, why did he not say so, at Mr.
Howson's? And again, when his father read the professor's letter?

Philip remembered Max had blushed and gone absolutely
silent, when Mr. Rochester told him about the soldiers. Did Max
know these were the Brontës's soldiers? But how could he know?
Anyway Max knew more than he was saying, Philip decided.

Either he had to work on his own, and write to this Seneca D.

Five Thousand Pounds

Brewer himself in secret; or he had to ingratiate himself with Max, and be let into whatever it was Max knew. (He had an idea Jane was in it.) And to get Max to let him into it was difficult when he had flung his brother off on to the attic floor as hard as he jolly well could.

Could it be done through Janey? This was possible. And meanwhile, *what* did Max know? Really there was no proving these were the very soldiers, there never would be, as his father had said, and they had not even been found at Haworth.

But did that matter? If this professor wanted to think they were, why not let him? If he was really silly enough to pay five thousand pounds for some old wooden soldiers, then it was likely he was sufficiently gullible to accept any that were offered.

No, Philip decided, the chance was much too good to be lost, and he had better get in first before anyone else offered theirs. He slammed the book to and swung out of bed with his mind made up. He returned the volume to Max's room, while Max was out of it, and as soon as breakfast was over, he bicycled to the post office, purchased an air-mail letter and wrote a suitable epistle to Professor Seneca D. Brewer.

From this it can be seen that Philip was a clear-sighted boy of acumen and determination, and when he did this he was thinking quite honestly how good it would be for Max (to say nothing of the rest of them, who might share a little in his fortune) to acquire the reward; and that even if he thought now that he cared more for the soldiers than the money he would not still think so in a few years' time.

But as yet Philip did not know the whole story.

Up in Max's bedroom, Max was telling Jane of last night's adventure. The book lay between them on the bed, and later they meant to read it.

"And I'd jolly well like to cut all the strings in his tennis racquet, or puncture his bike," Max finished venomously, still feeling sore over Philip's behaviour.

"Well look, Max, the chief thing is that Butter and the others weren't *hurt*," Jane said, "but I *do* think we ought to protect them more."

"So do I. Butter said that as they did not recognize the Monster they all remained frozen. But will they always be quick enough to do that? Do you think I ought to warn Butter to tell them to? Supposing Mummy and Daddy ask to see them again, because of this old professor's letter? And what if someone goes in the attic, and they're doing things?"

"Yes, or looks through the keyhole, while we're in there. Max, do you think Philip's going to do anything?"

"What could he do?"

"He could write to that professor, couldn't he, and tell him about your soldiers?"

"But he'd ask Daddy and Mummy first, wouldn't he?" Max said, horrified.

Jane looked doubtful.

"We *could* hide them somewhere, if we had to," she said.

This idea comforted Max, and he felt very glad that he had Jane to help him. They went up to the attic, found that the door had a rusty bolt inside (perhaps it was once a bedroom) and made this work by using the bicycle oil. Jane also found a small piece of wood to fill up the keyhole from inside. There was no key.

With these precautions taken they felt happier.

"Max," Jane now said, turning to an idea she had thought of last night in bed, "can I make them a feast?"

Max stared at her. It sounded suspiciously like a doll's tea-party.

"But, Jane, you can't *play* with them. Like that," he protested.

"I didn't mean play with them," she said. "I only meant put it all ready, and see if they like it——"

"You mustn't sit them up, or anything, they'd probably be offended," he explained.

"I know, I wasn't going to. But you fed them, you said so, when they were on the kitchen table. After all, you've done lots of things with them, seeing them get downstairs and all that, and I haven't done any."

Jane, being a girl, was really perhaps more interested in feeding the Twelves than seeing them on parade.

"Oh, all right, it can't hurt to put it ready, I s'pose," Max said.

"I know, I'll make a great table, like at a banquet, while you get the things."

"Yes," said Jane, and she slipped out, and hurried downstairs.

Max fetched his bricks and laid some in a row. Over these he put an old Snakes and Ladders board folded up. Round this imposing table he put more bricks, enough to seat the Young Men. At the head of the table he built a more splendid seat than the rest, higher, and with a back and arms. This he intended for the patriarch.

"But," muttered Max, "I shouldn't be surprised if one of those four kings doesn't pinch it."

So he put four second best seats each side of the patriarch, two a side. These had backs, but no arms. They were meant for the kings. The seats below them each side were simply single bricks with no backs or arms and were meant for the other soldiers.

"I hope they'll know what I mean," Max said to himself. All this took a good deal of fiddling, to find the right-sized bricks, and when Jane came back Max had only just finished.

"That's super," she whispered. And she began quickly to lay upon the table the set of tiny brass plates she had kept from her dolls' house days. At either end, she put a brass candlestick, and between these, small piled plates, gleaming at the edge, filled with bread crumbs, cake crumbs, biscuit crumbs, desiccated cocoanut, currants, and silver pills. The plates were milk bottle tops. By each man's own plate she put a tiny wine glass. Finally, quite aware that the Twelves would expect strong drink and not tea, she put a decanter each end, filled with a rich red drink.

Max was delighted. Fancy Jane having kept all the wine glasses and decanters, unbroken! She had had them years ago. He had broken the stem from one, but his mother had carefully stuck it back. It was true, what Jane said about girls being careful with their things.

When the feast was spread, the Genius Janeii retired modestly to the other end of the attic and waited. Max picked up the patriarch, who all this time had sat motionless with the others in the canoe.

"The Genii have spread you a table in the wilderness," he said,

Five Thousand Pounds

"partake if you choose." And as he said it, he reminded himself of the twenty-third psalm, though he could not quite think why. It seemed a suitable way of telling Butter Crashey, who at once bowed and showed every sign of pleasure. Max put him back and sat on the Ashanti stool.

The Twelves were not long in accepting the invitation. They fixed a balsa wood gang plank, and scrambled or slid down it, according to taste, running for seats at the table as if they had not seen a banquet for years, which was indeed the case. The younger members, notably the middies Crackey, Tracky and Monkey, elbowed and pushed and squealed with excitement, the more stalwart warriors took their middle places with greater ceremony, while the four kings and the patriarch himself walked in a solemn procession from the boat. Sneaky strutted with such an air of conceited haughtiness, and yawned with such a bored flourish of his hand to his mouth, that it made Max laugh. But he could not help noticing that their walk became brisk as they neared their places.

They ate, drank, talked, choked, laughed, toasted, slapped each other on the back and grew very merry as befitted such gallant Young Men.

Bravey, indeed, so far forgot himself as to leap up on his seat, and beginning to jump wildly in the air and wave his arms, sang in a loud voice:

> *"Cannikin clink*
> *Drink, boys, drink,*
> *Drink, drink,*
> *Cannikin clink."*

This song, evidently well-known to the rest, caused immense excitement. The decanters were seized and passed round, glasses clinked, more than one Young Man followed Bravey's example and stood upon his chair, Sneaky dancing so wildly and jumping so high in the air that it seemed doubtful to Max whether he would land upon the seat again, and more likely that the table would be upset, and Jane's wine-glasses broken beyond repair. The patriarch, however, called them to order, and the wild junketing gave place to brave stories and loud laughter. When not a crumb

84

Five Thousand Pounds

was left, not a drop of ruby red liquid, and when several were showing distinct signs of inebriation, the patriarch arose.

Max leaned forward eagerly to hear what he would say, and Jane crawled a little nearer.

"Beware, Young Men, of all Monsters such as he who seized upon us recently. Show no signs of life to any but the two Genii you know. This warning came to me from the present Chief Genii. An unknown danger threatens the Twelves." And with this the patriarch held up his hands and took his splendid seat again. The bell rang for lunch. Max and Jane tiptoed from the attic.

"When did you warn Butter?" she said. "About Philip?"

"I didn't. Only in my mind, I was going to," Max said. "But he seems to know. He said it to me once, he said that the chief Genii said: 'Revere this man Crashey, he is entrusted with secrets which you can never know.' "

"So we needn't worry too much," Jane said, "only keep our eyes open."

Their father had the local paper by his plate.

Five Thousand Pounds

"I said that professor's letter would raise a dust," he laughed. "Listen to this one.

"Sir,

In the unlikely event of the set of Brontë soldiers to which Professor Seneca D. Brewer refers in his letter, coming to light, it is to be hoped that the owner or finder will know his local, nay, his national duty, and will offer them to the Brontë museum. This is their rightful home, and we in this part of Yorkshire are their rightful guardians. It would be monstrous if this unexpected remnant of the Brontë heritage should cross the Atlantic.

I remain, Sir, etc., etc.,

So cross, and they're not even found yet," said Mr. Morley, laughing.

"Isn't it priceless, how they keep saying, 'Nay'," remarked Philip, lightly.

"I wonder if the museum will weigh in," said Mrs. Morley.

"Will they offer to pay the £5,000 for them?" asked Jane. "Instead?"

"There's no knowing," said her father. "Maxy, shall we write to the old professor, and say you've got them?" he suggested, half-teasing. "And get the £5,000?"

Max's pixie face went white. He swallowed his mouthful.

"No," he said fiercely. "They're mine, I found them, I don't want five thousand pounds, you *can't!*"

Chapter 13

The Battle
of Atticum

In the next few days Max and Jane spent more time with the
Twelves than with the rest of the family. For one thing, the fine
hot weather had, for the moment, broken: and Mrs. Morley,
still busy with all the details of settling into the new house, hardly
noticed how much they were in the attic. For another, Jane had
become as enslaved to the Young Men as Max, but in a rather
different way. It was Jane who first said that they should pick up
and speak to each Young Man, that they should get to know them
separately. For a third, all the fuss about the American professor
seemed to have died down, their father had said no more, and
Philip had been particularly nice to Max, as if he were trying to
atone for the fight in the attic.

It was Jane who noticed that Crackey, aged five, had indeed in
his wooden state, a crack in the back of his head beneath his hat.

"And how did you get that, Crackey?" Jane whispered.

" 'it by a cannon ball and never 'ealed up," replied Crackey
promptly and proudly.

And it was Jane who saw that Tracky, aged ten, his friend, was
for ever following people about and tracking them down. When he
managed to take them by surprise he would fling his arms round
them and shout, "Got you". Very much as Max sometimes did.
She also noticed that Tracky was a particular gad-fly to the sober
King Parry: the two were evidently enemies of long-standing, and
she wondered what old quarrel lay behind it.

Jane observed too how like a tiny ape's was the bright-eyed,
snubby face of Monkey, and he behaved like a monkey as well,
climbing up everything he could find, in the way which he must

have learned when he was a midshipman on the *Invincible.*

"And you know, Jane," Max said, "they're all beastly to poor old Gravey. I know he's gloomy and never smiles, but whenever he opens his mouth they sneer at him."

"Yes, and he often falls over, because he's either nervous or he's absent-minded or something, and then they all laugh," she added, for she had seen this too.

"I don't wonder he's sour, like Branwell says in the story, do you. Perhaps if you were to spoil him a bit he'd feel better?" Max suggested.

As for the volatile Sneaky, he was often to be seen playing tricks upon the rest, sneaking up on them, tripping them over, blowing down their necks, and then looking the other way, and generally behaving in the most unkingly fashion. Then he would as suddenly go into a mood and look haughty and dark, and hide in some corner by himself, and sneer at anyone who came to talk to him, and make bitter remarks about his fate. He was certainly, as Jane said, a strange mixture. The other two kings, Parry and Ross, were more straightforward and dignified but very ingenious. Parry was tall and spare, Ross was shorter and broader, and seemed the most open in the way he behaved. It was often they who led the rest on clambering expeditions in the attic. Over mountains of books, up to the plateaux of trunks and furniture, they went, looking down from these dizzy heights to piles of folded curtains below, crossing a glacier (which was a mirror not yet in use) and from there jumping into a soft snowdrift of spare blankets. When they did these things Max and Jane had to watch them carefully in case one should get left behind and lost.

Now one morning the telegraph boy came whistling up to the Morleys' door and knocked loudly. Philip, who had been lurking around the house the last day or two almost as if he were expecting something of the kind, darted out of the drawing-room, opened the door, and took in a cablegram.

This he at once began to open, while telling the boy there would be no answer at the moment.

"How d'you know it's for you?" Jane asked, on her way to do an errand for her mother.

"Because it says so," growled Philip, disappearing again.

But now that he had done it, now that his letter had reached the professor, and the professor had answered, Philip felt worried and uneasy. How was he to tell Max? How was he to persuade Max this was all for his good? What would his mother and father say? And what would all those cross people who wrote to the paper say, if the soldiers left England? Philip read the message again.

"Flying to England fifteenth to inspect wooden soldiers.

BREWER."

Philip chewed the back of his knuckles, and then flicked his fingers, standing first on one foot and then on the other.

And would Seneca D. Brewer expect to be entertained by Mrs. Morley? And what would Mrs. Morley think of this?

Philip often referred to his mother as Mrs. Morley; it was a kind of joke, used when he needed anything very badly, or had something to confess. He now wandered out to the kitchen, looking vacant on purpose, and said:

"Mrs. Morley."

"Hullo, darling, what do you want?" she said at once.

Philip handed her the form.

"What's this?" she said, taking it with a floury hand.

"Philip, do you mean you wrote to him?" she said.

Philip nodded, still looking vacant, his eyes fixed on a far corner of the ceiling.

"But what did you tell him?"

"Just how Max had found them and that they go with the ones in *The History of the Young Men*."

"But does Max know, does he agree? You heard what he said to Daddy."

"He doesn't know."

"Well, Philip, whatever made you do it, when you heard what Max said?" she asked.

"I'd already done it." ·

His mother was silent, for she could not help admiring his prompt efficiency. She supposed he had compared the soldiers with the description in the book. On the other hand, it was no joke to bring a professor flying over the Atlantic, only to find a small boy would not part with some wooden soldiers. She said so.

"I know," Philip said gloomily, "but surely he'll see reason. After all, five thousand pounds!"

"Phil, you know what kind of a boy Max is, money means nothing to him yet, why should it? Also, how can anyone possibly tell?" she said crossly. "There's no proof they're the ones, such things were made in thousands, how can we take all that money from a crazy scholar who's let an idea run away with him?"

"That's his look out. But you know what Max calls them? Don't you remember that first day, he called them the Twelves? And you said what is the Twelves? I remember distinctly. And have you forgotten, one's Butter, aged 140, and one's Stumps? It's all in that book you know. How did Max *know*?"

"Well, he and Jane have been reading the book."

"Mrs. Morley," Philip said in some exasperation, "it was all *before* you produced the book. You wouldn't do for a detective. Max knows something, more than he's saying."

"What *do* you mean, Philip, how could he? He brought that old roll of rag with them inside, straight down, quite openly, to show us all."

"All the same, I swear he's got some clue those soldiers belonged to the Brontës. Well, what shall I do?" he said, appealingly, as if he were Max's age again.

"You must go up and tell him what you've done. You've got yourself into it, Phil, you must simply go and tell him, and see what he thinks. He may be willing to part with them. You ought to prevent this poor man coming if he's not. You're not to bully and upset Max, now."

Philip went slowly upstairs, working out a plan of campaign as carefully as a general works out a battle.

Meanwhile Max was alone in the attic, absorbed in another battle. He had put out the chess men, in a cohort, as if they were a rival army, for he had just read in Branwell's story how he had let the Twelves fight some cannibal ninepins. Sure enough, the Young Men had at once taken them for an army, and had prepared for battle. The Duke of Wellington, Bravey, Ross and Parry had dragged Max's bag of marbles over the attic floor, and every man was seizing on these glittering cannon balls and bowling them with a noise like small thunder across the attic floor at the chessmen. Whenever a man was hit there was a howl of glee, and if he were hit three times he was pushed ignominiously from the field. Tracky was acting as ball boy, returning the cannon-balls which missed, Monkey was beating the Ashanti drum with the balsa

wood, and the Duke was standing on a pedestal made of two drafts, the flag planted beside him, urging his men on. The best shots were undoubtedly Stumps, Cheeky, Parry and Ross. Sneaky was too excited to aim straight: but Gravey was extremely good, as he kept his eye on the job and never wavered or took time off to ask the rest to admire him.

Meanwhile, Butter had wanted to be picked up, and he now surveyed the battle of Atticum, as Max called it, from Max's hand, his two arms held aloft, like Moses in the Bible, as if he were holding up the good cause of the Twelves.

Max heard Philip's tread, thought that the attic door was bolted, remembered Jane had gone out, and sprang to his feet too late.

The attic door was opened, even as Max hissed, "Monster!" Butter Crashey was still waving his arms wildly as Philip came in, and in a quick instinctive movement to hide him, Max plunged him into his pocket, keeping his fingers on him.

The battle had frozen. Some soldiers feigned dead. One solitary marble went rumbling away past Monkey at the drum into the far corner of the attic.

"Hullo," Philip said pleasantly.

"Hullo," said Max cautiously. And he sat down on the Ashanti stool, his hand gently round Butter Crashey in his pocket.

"Maxy," began Philip, and as he spoke he picked up—who was it?—it was Max's darling Stumps (as Jane called him). He held him with great care and consideration, however, looking at him off and on.

"You know that professor," he went on, "who wrote to the paper about the soldiers?"

"Yes," said Max. And his heart gave a great, uncontrolled *wumph*, like the noise of the drum.

"Well, you don't think it would hurt, do you, for him to come and see these soldiers? Just to look at them, and see if he thinks they're the ones he wants?" Philip wheedled.

"I don't care whether he wants them or not," Max replied going straight to the point, "he's not going to have them, so what's the use of him coming to see them?"

"But if they ARE the right ones," Philip went on, "he'll give you five thousand pounds for them, think how useful it would be! Smashing, Max, you'll be able to get all sorts of things you want. And after all, if he takes them to America, they'll be terribly well looked after. They have the most marvellous museums and collections and things in America. They can't come to any harm."

"They're not going to America," said Max, "because I'm not selling them."

"Well it's not really selling, it's a kind of reward for finding them. You know, you won't want to play with them, in a few more years, I promise you."

"I don't play with them now," said Max with dignity.

Philip smiled.

"And anyway," he said, "if it once gets known you've got them, they'll want them at Haworth, at the Brontë Museum, you won't be allowed to keep them here, I bet Mummy and Daddy won't let you. Haworth is where they used to be, if they are really Branwell's. The Genii Brannii," he added. "Good, isn't it? That story?"

"Mummy said," Max replied stubbornly, "that nobody could possibly prove they are the ones, so therefore the museum can't take them."

Philip was silent a moment.

"But *you* think they are, don't you?" he said next, trying it on.

Max held on to Butter rather tightly, and said nothing. His eyes were on Stumps, who was being waved through the air rather a lot, enough to cause him to swoon or be sick, Max thought. He hoped Stumps was safely frozen.

"You *do*, don't you, Maxy?"

Still Max said nothing.

"I wonder why," Philip said, trying to draw him out. "Anyway," he said briskly, and feeling slightly ashamed, because he was up against something he did not understand, "this professor's coming. Just to see them. It can't hurt."

"But how does he know I've got them?" Max said, unable to believe what was obvious.

"Because I've told him," leered Philip, teasing. He leered because now he was ashamed, properly, feeling Max's seriousness and distress.

"But I told Daddy not to, I said I didn't want him to write," Max said in the utmost consternation.

"I wrote. Before you ever said that," Philip said.

"You are a beast." Philip did not look at him, for he was afraid his eyes were full of tears.

"But I thought you'd be pleased to get the money. When you'd thought it over," Philip said, "so I just did it. Look, this is what he says."

Max read the cable.

The Battle of Atticum

"I'm sorry you're cross," Philip said, putting on a slightly hurt voice. "I thought you'd be pleased."

"But you don't understand," Max said helplessly, stroking Butter with one finger. He held out the other hand and took Stumps from his brother. Then he turned away and went over to the attic window, which was open, and put Stumps on the sill, and looked out over the moors.

"Oh well," Philip said, and shrugged his shoulders, "you can always say no, if you're so silly." And he went out, relieved that it was over.

Chapter 14

Gone

Each morning Mr. Morley would seize upon the local paper and turn to the correspondence to see if there were any more letters about the soldiers. There was a lull after the first day or two, and then they started again.

"Now, that's exactly what I think," said their father with satisfaction, reading a letter. "It's what I said, you remember." Everybody likes having his own opinion backed up and Mr. Morley sounded very pleased.

"What is?" said Philip.

"Read it, Daddy," urged Jane. "Is it a new one about the soldiers?"

"Yes. 'Sir,' read her father, crackling the paper in his square, brown hands, 'it is surely infantile to suppose that the cause of serious literary criticism, or even of serious biography, however psychologically slanted, can possibly be furthered by the examination of some wooden toys, of a kind made by the thousand, and played with in their childhood by the Brontë family. What they imagined and wrote about these soldiers is perhaps valuable and certainly revealing. Much of it is published and available. To think the toys themselves would be illuminating is only sentimental. I remain, etc.,' I hope Seneca D. Brewer reads that," he finished.

Max sat up with a jerk, and his eyes glittered, as he looked at Jane. There were a great many hard words in the letter, yet he thought he had the sense of it. The soldiers, being wooden and like many others, could not tell anybody anything. How little these people knew about the venerable Crashey, the Duke of Wellington, dear Stumps, lively Sneaky, bold Cheeky, gloomy Gravey, hard-

95

drinking Bravey, Monkey and the middies! He looked at his father, smiling. Mr. Morley thought that Max was pleased because the letter meant that his soldiers were less in danger of being pursued, and put in a museum. So he winked and said:

"That'll settle Seneca, eh, Max?"

And then a silence fell upon the table, because Mr. Morley was the only one who did not yet know that the professor was proposing to fly the Atlantic, and bear down upon them. Mr. Morley saw his family exchange glances.

"Go on, Philip," said his mother. "Tell."

"What?" said Philip's father, startled.

"Seneca's coming," Philip said, enjoying the sensation he was causing. And he took the cablegram from his pocket and pushed it at his father.

"Philip, you are a young idiot," Mr. Morley said, crossly, when he had realized what it meant.

"Daddy, *you* suggested writing yourself. Actually I'd already done it," said Philip, his voice rising high with injury and protest, "but you know you did."

"What are we going to do?" said Mr. Morley to his wife.

"I don't know," she said resignedly. "Maxy won't part with them, there's no proving they're the ones, the whole thing is ridiculous. But it's not our fault, the man must have money to burn. I've told Philip he ought to put him off."

"Philip, you must have given him the impression they're the Brontë soldiers, if he's willing to fly to see them," said Mr. Morley gloomily, turning for consolation to the paper again. "Here's another letter, all about the horrors of war, and how boys shouldn't be allowed to play with soldiers. That'll be from one of the Friends."

Now Yorkshire has its share of those who call themselves Friends, or Quakers, and they disapprove strongly of anything to do with war. They themselves will never be soldiers or fight in any way, they will only help the victims. Should anything which glorifies war, asked this Friend, even a set of wooden soldiers who inspired the imaginations of the four Brontës, be allowed to be so important as to cause a hue and cry, and the offer of a huge reward?

Gone

Give your five thousand pounds, he told the professor sternly, to the refugees, the guiltless victims of the last terrible war and those oppressions which followed it.

"Well, I must say I can agree with him," said their mother.

"There'll be answers to both of those, I expect," Mr. Morley said.

And it was not only through the paper that the interest in the Brontë soldiers grew, it soon became clear that people in the neighbourhood were beginning to know of the Morley's possible part in the affair. Bill, for instance, Mr. Morley's help on the farm, said with curiosity:

"It's a rum 'un what it says in t' paper, about them toy soldiers that Brontë bairns had! Happen it's your little lad that's found them?"

Mr. Morley was taken by surprise and hedged.

"But there can't be any proof whatever that any soldiers found here are anything to do with the Brontës, Bill, how could there be?"

And he thought to himself, how did *Bill* know, has Maxy told him?

"But folks is saying that some professor's bahnd ovver 'ere, all t' road from America, nobbut just to see 'em," Bill asked in a questioning tone.

And Mr. Morley realized then that of course it might have leaked out about the cable, and no wonder it had caused talk. Why should they not be interested? They were reading their paper like everyone else.

The baker, coming up to the kitchen door, said cheerfully to Mrs. Morley:

"Nay, Missis, it caps all, what they say these 'ere wooden soldiers'll fetch! By, but I wouldn't mind finding 'em me-sen, I can tell you that!"

Mrs. Morley could not tell from this whether he knew of Max's find or whether he had only read the paper, so she said that she expected the fuss would all die down soon.

But Jane, who had overheard both these things and had discreetly said nothing at all, ran up quickly to the attic where Max was.

"Angria," she whispered, through the keyhole, tapping three

97

times. This was their password. They had found out from the book that the name which Branwell and Charlotte Brontë later gave to their imaginary country of the Young Men was Angria. "Instead of Africa, I suppose," Jane had said. So they had decided to use it for a password.

Max unbolted the door and Jane slipped inside.

"Maxy," she began anxiously, "everyone seems to know about them. Bill's just said to Daddy he hears you may be the lucky finder. And the baker said something about them to Mummy——"

Max interrupted her.

"Who's told Bill? Philip?"

"I asked Mummy that. She says she expects it may be because of the cable arriving. Where are they all, anyway?" she whispered.

"They've gone on a climbing trip. Over Daddy's rucksack, can you see? Ross used the cord to pull himself up, and now they're all doing it, look." Jane looked and saw a line of the Young Men, pulling themselves up the steep, grey wrinkled slopes of the rucksack by the cord which hung from its neck. Ross, Sneaky and the Duke had reached the top, jumped over the edge and were peering out as if it were a great crater. The rucksack was full of camping stuff and there was a groundsheet folded at the top.

"They're so ingenious," she said.

"Yes. *And* brave," added Max. "After all, it might be a volcano for all they probably know."

"Maxy, what *are* we going to do, when this professor arrives?" Jane said, when they had watched the mountaineers a little longer. Gravey had just stumbled over a slippery bulge, and was swinging by the rope. A wave of thin, jeering laughter could be heard from the slope, and even the Duke, from the edge of the crater, was smiling. As for Sneaky, he was doubled-up with laughter.

"Never mind, Gravey darling," said Jane in a gentle whisper. "The Genii love and protect you."

And at this Gravey renewed his foothold and climbed on, his sad face full of determination.

"I don't know about the professor, that's what I've been trying to think out. I want Mummy to stop him coming. And the only thing I can think of is to let her into the secret."

"What I'm afraid of is that if we tell a grown-up, they'll say it can't be true and the Twelves will freeze for ever."

"I know, that's what I thought. It would have to be a special kind of a person, who understood. Surely if they saw them alive they couldn't say it wasn't true? And then they'd help us protect them."

"Yes, Mummy would know how to put everyone off."

"Or should we just hide them, Jane, put them somewhere away from here, in their box?"

"Max, they'd *hate* it!"

And together they wondered how they could possibly explain to Butter Crashey and the rest that they must for the moment be buried alive again.

"Of course, they'd freeze then all right," said Max.

"Yes, and they might never come back to life," Jane added.

"We could explain it would be no worse than being under the floor board, and we'd rescue them again when it was safe. I wondered if the Howsons would mind if we used their grotto right behind, in the little cave? Nobody would look there," Max suggested.

"Do we want to tell the Howsons? I say, Maxy, what about Mr. Howson, Mr. Rochester? *He'd* be interested, he'd believe in them, and help us!" Jane said, suddenly.

Max nodded. He had promised to show Mr. Howson the soldiers. Mr. Howson was a brontyfan and knew all about the Young Men.

"I bet he's been reading the letters in the paper," Max said.

At this minute they heard their mother's step on the stair, and her voice calling.

"Maxy! Jane! Are you in the attic?"

"Yes," they answered, springing up.

"Well, Max, there's a reporter ringing up from the paper, asking about the soldiers. Open the door, darling, I don't want to have to shout. Why do you keep the door bolted?" And Mrs. Morley, not unnaturally impatient, wiggled the handle.

"I'm coming out," Max said hastily, and did so.

"This man wants to know whether it's true that one of my sons has found some soldiers like the Brontë ones, and can he come and interview the finder, and photograph him with his find?"

"It's all those letters," Max scowled. "Who *told* them?"

"Darling, I don't know. What am I to say, he's holding on?"

"But did you tell him it was true?" Max demanded.

"No, I said I wondered how he'd heard that, and that I'd come and ask you."

Max looked at his mother gratefully.

"Well, say NO, Mummy," he ordered.

"You won't give an interview. Doesn't it sound grand? And what about photographing the soldiers?"

"No, no, no," Max said in terror. "They don't want to be in the paper, nor do I, Mummy."

Mrs. Morley thought how different Max was from other boys, who might rather like being in the paper. And again she wondered at his fierce and secret attachment to these soldiers.

"I'm afraid they'll make up a story if we don't give them one, but I'll just say no, and ring off," she said. "Is Janey there?"

"Yes. Thank you, Mummy," Max said, "I do think Phil's a beast, it's all his fault, about the cable," he blurted.

"It's all rather nonsense, in my view," she said, and she wanted to ask: Max, what is it, about these soldiers? *They don't want to be in the paper*, he had said. But she remembered the reporter, holding on, and hurried downstairs.

"Jane," Max said going back into the attic. "Did you hear? It's getting *dangerous*!"

"Yes, I did," Jane nodded.

And in the afternoon the reporter did not bother to ring up again, he simply came. Jane and Max stampeded to the attic, and bolted the door. They heard their mother repeat again and again that she had nothing to say. Not long after this Mr. Howson telephoned Mr. Morley, saying he was so interested to read all this in the paper, and he could not help connecting it with Max's soldiers and could he possibly come and see them tomorrow? Mr. Morley naturally said Yes.

Jane and Max, on the way to bed, decided that they would let Mr. Howson see the Twelves, and that if the time seemed right, they would warn Butter Crashey, and present the noble patriarch, lively and wise, to the parson; and ask for his advice as an elder Genii.

When they had decided this, they felt happier. Max said they could always, after all, tell their mother too, for she had been marvellous with the reporter.

The next morning, when they went up to get the Young Men ready in ranks, for inspection, not a soldier was in sight.

"Oh, they've mountaineered, somewhere," Max said, beginning to search.

"Yes, I expect so," Jane answered, joining in.

They searched high, they searched low, under, inside, back of beyond. They searched more and more quickly, and loudly, bumping into each other, with fear growing inside them.

"Jane, in the rucksack!"

"No. Max, in that roll of carpet!"

"No. In their box?"

"No. Max, under their old floor board?"

Max dived for the squeaky board, scrabbled frantically at it, lifted it up. Empty. Put his hands right in, as far as they would go. Dirt and cobwebs.

"No!" Max was almost crying and Jane was pale.

"They've gone!" she said at last, clutching her hands over her chest.

Lost? Not lost in the attic, they had searched. And the door had been safely shut at night. Stolen?

The window was open. They often had it open, and seldom bothered to shut it in dry weather. It was wide open this morning.

Or strayed?

Who could tell?

Max flopped over the Ashanti stool.

"We haven't protected them," he sobbed. "We've let them be taken. What will happen to them?"

Chapter 15

Where?

"Max! Jane!" called Mrs. Morley, up the attic stairs. "Can you bring the soldiers down, or must Mr. Howson climb up?"

"Maxy!" Jane said, shaking his shoulder gently. "He's here. Mr. Howson. Stop crying, Max. Coming, Mummy," she called from the door.

But she knew what Max was thinking, he was thinking how puzzled and hurt the patriarch and the Duke and the others would be to be treated as wooden, and with no thoughts or feelings. She was thinking the same herself, she was wondering about Crackey-aged-five, and Monkey, and poor melancholy Gravey, whose spirits she always had to encourage by loving him especially. Who had taken them? Who was turning them over now, and looking at them, and putting them head first in a box somewhere?

"Max, we'll have to go. Come on," she said going to the attic door.

"Stumps sings songs," remarked Max miserably, getting up and scrubbing at his eyes. And the thought of Stumps's brave climb made his tears start again.

Side by side they went down the attic stairs, slowly and soberly. Max ran his hands down the banisters.

"Their string," he sniffed, noticing it and remembering the adventurous descent.

"We'll find them, I expect. Mummy'll think of something," said Jane.

They presented themselves at the drawing-room door. Jane

smiled a faint and sad smile and the traces of Max's tears still showed.

"Hullo, I mean, good morning," Jane said.

"Good morning, Jane and Max," Mr. Howson replied. Their father came in from the garden.

"Where are these famous soldiers, now?" he said. "I'm quite looking forward to seeing them again myself. Max monopolizes them in the attic, you know," he explained.

"Didn't you bring them down, Jane?" said her mother. "What's the matter?"

"They're not there," Jane said.

"They've gone," sniffed Max.

The three adults stared at the children, trying to fathom the meaning of the distress on their faces.

"You mean you've lost them? The whole lot, this time?" said their father.

"They were there last night, we haven't lost them," Jane said, "they just aren't *there*, now. Mummy, the window was open," Jane finished, helplessly.

"Max," said his father, "you haven't hidden them, have you?" he asked; for his wife had been describing to him Max's intense attachment to the soldiers, and he wondered if Max was unwilling to show them to Mr. Howson, and whether poor Jane was shielding Max.

"No," Max said, "I haven't."

And he looked at Mr. Howson, who understood the expression on his face and said quickly:

"I'm sure he hasn't," and did not smile.

"Jane, d'you mean you think someone may have stolen them?" her mother asked.

"The window was open, you see. And you know the creeper comes right up," Jane said.

"You know, with this idea in the paper of their being worth five thousand pounds, it's quite possible, isn't it?" said Mr. Morley. "That someone would try to take them?"

"More than possible, I'm afraid, I thought of it at once," said the parson.

Where?

"But, Roderick, how could anyone know where they were? Or which was the attic? Anyway, it's a very high, dangerous climb!" Mrs. Morley remarked. "Have you looked up?"

"Things get about. Let's go and inspect," said their father, at once.

They went out of the back door and stood in a row, looking up at the open attic window and the creeper.

"He'd have the pipe to help, part of the way," Mrs. Morley said.

"Look, if someone's been up the creeper there'll be broken branches and twigs," said Mr. Morley firmly and he went to examine it. There was not a broken twig or crushed leaf or bruised patch of bark anywhere, so far as they could see. The paint on the pipe was unscratched.

And as Max looked up, he thought of Stumps, and an idea came into his head.

"It's more likely someone who has the run of the house," said the parson. "Perhaps?" he added, for this seemed a nasty thing to suggest.

"But no one sleeps in, I only have my daily, and there's Bill——" said Max's mother.

"Bill helps me. He knows, he spoke of it to me. But I don't distrust Bill."

Then Mrs. Morley said: "Oh Jane, have you asked Philip? Philip may have taken them, borrowed them, put them safely somewhere, ready for this professor! Have you heard, Mr. Howson, the American professor may be coming?"

"I did hear a rumour to that effect, in your village. I was rather upset at the idea of their going to America."

"They're not going," Max said furiously. "Where's Philip, I'll *kill* him if he's taken them——"

"Max, Max, don't be so violent, he can't hurt them," Mrs. Morley said.

And at this minute, Philip circled into the yard on his bicycle.

Max dashed at him, and seized the handlebars.

"Where are the soldiers? Have you taken the soldiers?" he screamed angrily.

"Of course I haven't, why should I?" Philip replied, also angry, because he knew Max was hurt about what he had done. And if you have injured another person it is hard to be decent to him.

"How do you do, Mr. Howson," he added, in his most grown-up manner.

"They've gone," announced Jane.

"Someone's pinched them, for the five thousand," Philip said at once.

And then everybody began explaining why this was so difficult.

"Look here," said Mr. Morley at last to Mr. Howson, "do you think I ought to tell the police? Just how valuable are they? *Are* they worth all that money? Are they historically interesting enough to be at Haworth? In other words, ARE they the Brontës's soldiers?"

"But I haven't seen them, you see," said Mr. Howson. "It's an artificial value, of course, but if there were proof they were, this man's willing to pay that much. That's what gives them value to the general public. If *I* thought they were Branwell's I would want to put them in the Haworth museum," he finished. "Of course."

Mr. Morley looked at Philip.

"You've seen them lately, Phil, and read the description in the book. What do you think? Do I tell the police?"

"Ask Max," Philip said. "Max thinks they're the Brontë ones. Jane does too, I believe."

"Do you, Max?"

Max looked cornered. He was quite agile enough in mind to see what was coming. He looked at Jane, as if for help.

"Yes," he said at last.

"Why?" said his father, and he sounded fiercer than he was, because he was puzzled.

"Just tell us why, Maxy," said his mother. But Max said nothing.

"Did you find something with them, that gave you the idea?" she went on, gently.

"No. You saw the bit of rag they were in."

"Have you found anything else in the attic?" asked his father, "to do with the Brontës?"

"No," said Max dully.

"Well, what gave you the idea of calling them the Twelves? And those names, Butter and Stumps?" Philip asked, joining in the questioning.

"I can't explain," Max said.

"Do you know, Jane?"

"Yes, but I can't explain," she said.

Mr. Morley looked explosive, and was probably only restrained from blowing up by the presence of the parson.

"We can do nothing to help you get them back unless you tell us all you know," he said. "I can't go to the police about any old wooden soldiers, Max, but I *can* go to them about the Brontë soldiers, for which America will pay five thousand and for which Haworth will soon be clamouring. Do you see?"

Max saw.

"I don't want you to go to the police," he said.

And in the pause which followed this a motor-car was heard turning into the yard. It was the reporter. Max drew in his breath, but nobody else said anything. The reporter got out of his motor-car and walked over to this silent group of people and his step became rather timid as he approached. Jane was sorry for the reporter, and when he smiled as if he were happy, and she knew he was not, she smiled back in sympathy.

"I'm sorry to intrude," he began, "but I wondered if the young man who found the Brontë soldiers had changed his mind."

Mr. Morley turned all his puzzled rage upon the poor reporter.

"I don't know where you heard that my son had found any soldiers," he said, "but there is no proof that the ones he found were anything to do with the Brontës, and there's no question of your seeing them, as they have now disappeared."

"Disappeared," said the reporter, smelling a good story. "Stolen? After all, five thousand pounds——"

"We do not think it likely, and I've no more to say. So will you please keep the thing out of the paper?"

But the reporter thought it more than likely, because it was a story.

"But where can they have gone if they haven't been stolen?" he said.

"I don't doubt," said Mr. Morley with irony, "that they have

climbed out of the window and walked off on their own. Good morning to you. Come along, Mr. Howson, come and have a drink, I'm more than sorry about all this," and he led the way to the house.

Max's eyes went bright again at his father's remark, and his mouth curled up; Jane looked quickly at the reporter and faintly blushed. Mr. Rochester noticed both these things, before he turned away with the Morleys, leaving the two younger children in the yard. The reporter gazed thoughtfully up at the house and the swinging attic window.

Chapter 16

The Thoughtful
Genii Maxii

"*That's* what it is, Janey!" Max said, "I thought of it at once, when Daddy said that the creeper would be crushed and broken! *They* wouldn't crush it, they're too light! Stumps knows the way, he's done it, as far as my room. And the attic window was open, and I stood Stumps on the sill! When I talked to Philip. And that would remind him. And, *Jane*, I've just thought, B. Crashey heard every word Philip said to me, about the professor and America, because he was in my pocket! He wasn't frozen, I had my hand on him, I could feel him move. He was listening, I expect!"

They had run off into the pig-garden, to avoid the reporter, who was still in the yard. They sat on some bales of straw at the far end, in a small Dutch barn.

"Wasn't it awful when Daddy *said* it? Did you see Mr. Rochester look at us? Do you mean, you think Butter knows they're in danger, and he's taken them to hide somewhere?" she answered.

"Yes. That's what I mean. You know about Butter having mysteries revealed to him that are hidden from the others," Max said.

"We may never find them again," remarked Jane sadly, "and I can't bear not to know what happens to them. I'd almost rather they went to America——"

"Oh *no*," Max said, "they ought to stay here."

"Max," Jane asked him, "how could they reach the attic window sill? It's quite high, you know."

"They'd swarm up my bit of string," Max said at once. "Don't you remember, there's a bit of string dangling from the window thing——"

"The hasp, you call it. Let's go and see. The reporter's gone, I heard his engine."

They ran, racing each other, over the pig-garden. It was like a detective game and they felt they must follow up every clue. They reached the attic, red and breathless, and dived for the window.

"There isn't any string, Maxy."

Max puffed and blew.

"There jolly well was," he said.

"You must have taken it off. How *could* they reach the sill, the stool's too far away, and they can't move things," Jane said.

"I know they climbed up the string," Max said stubbornly. "It's to do with imagining what they would do. I told you how I imagined how Stumps found Brutus's door, and he had, it was all true. I can't always do it, but I'm sure they went down the creeper, and I can't understand about the string. If I think hard tonight I may be able to see what they did."

Jane looked at Max, interested.

"It's almost as if what you imagine for them, they do, isn't it? It's almost as if you put the ideas into their heads, as if you were kind of . . . kind of . . . God, to them? This is what Genii means, I 'spose."

"It was, when I wanted Stumps to climb the creeper. Because just as I was thinking it, he did it. But this is the other way round, you see, because they've done it, they've gone, and I've got to imagine where."

They both leaned from the high dormer window and stared into the thick creeper.

"You know, they could be still hiding *in* it," said Jane.

"I bet they're not. Shall we search the pigs' place, and the garden, Jane?"

"Yes," she said, "let's, come on." She did not argue about the string. Even if Max was wrong about it, she felt, as he did, that the Young Men would find a way and that this was the way they had gone.

They searched most thoroughly round the yard and the garden.

The Thoughtful Genii Maxii

Max lay on his tummy and, shading his eyes, squinted under both the water butts. A toad's eyes glinted sleepily back at him from one. Jane searched in the garage, and the old stable, behind a pile of harness. They quartered the garden, peering under the overgrown borders and straggling fruit bushes (for the house had stood empty and the garden was neglected) and every minute expecting to see a little group of bright-eyed trembling Twelves, staring out in bold fear. Jane was careful not to be too wild and rough, for she could imagine how terrified they would be, and yet how determined to be brave, encouraged by the stout-hearted surgeon Cheeky. Max agreed.

There were all kinds of good places, he said. There was a proper underground palace beneath the laurel bush in the front garden, dry, lofty, and completely hidden. There was a rockery, also overgrown, with little caves where twelve Young Men could easily sit hidden. But they were not doing so.

"Let's try the barn, where the bales are," Jane suggested.

But the only occupant of the barn was Brutus, wedged in a good hole between two layers of bales. He yawned and began at once to purr.

"I hope they didn't meet Brutus," Max said.

"Brutus, where are the Twelves?" said Jane. Brutus gave no answer.

Near the big farm gate at the front, Max found one of his skates. He at once put it on and used it as a scooter, remembering he had left them there yesterday and wondering where the other was.

Mrs. Morley had noticed their search, and was puzzled by it. As they came across the yard, not knowing where to look next, but far from beaten, she called:

"What are you looking for, Maxy? You didn't play with the soldiers in the garden, did you?"

Max was thankful for the skate.

"Well, I've lost one of my skates," he said.

"We thought they might have got into the garden, Mummy," added Jane truthfully.

"Only if you put them there," she said. "What do you think has happened?" she went on, regarding her two children suspiciously.

"I still think they could have been pinched," Jane mumbled.

But Max clattered off on his one skate in order to avoid discussing it. It was too tricky.

"Of course, Jane," he said, "they might have gone much further. They may not be still on the farm at all."

"I know. But which direction shall we look?"

"We shall have to look in every direction there is, if we want to find them. But I tell you what, they won't walk about by day."

"No. They'll hide by day and walk by night, if they're going anywhere," she agreed.

"The further they go, the worse it is to find them," Max said, his eyes large. He felt that it was urgent to catch up with the Young Men at once. "If only I could imagine what's happened."

"Perhaps you can try tonight," suggested Jane. "It must be almost what people do who write stories, don't you think?"

"Well, that's what the Four Genii *did*!" Max replied.

In the afternoon they tried further afield, almost to the edge of the moors. The heather was an endless hiding place, for lizards, mice, grass snakes, or the Young Men. When Max went to bed, he felt that they might be anywhere amongst that wiry, purple forest and that he might never see them again. But he would never, never forget them. He could imagine them all quite clearly, even their tiny faces, as if he had only to go up to the attic and there they would all be. And he imagined what a bustle and excitement there must have been in the attic last night, when they were preparing to go.

He shut his eyes and he could see Butter Crashey, now, holding up his arms to the rest, saying: "Young Men, a fearful, unknown danger awaits us if we stay here. We are likely to be transported to an entirely different foreign clime. Uprooted from the moorland we know, which was beloved by our first Genii, we shall be put into a flying machine, helpless to resist, and not touch ground again until we have crossed thousands of miles of ocean. It is not that we cannot trust our present Genii"—(Max had to put this bit in, for he could not bear Butter Crashey to think he was treacherous)—"it is simply that they themselves may be powerless against bigger monsters. Prepare, oh Young Men; arm, Twelves, for we must flee!"

The Thoughtful Genii Maxii

"As to arms," remarked the Duke rather cynically, "we have none, we must find them on the way. How are the mighty fallen and the weapons of war perished. Not a bayonet remains."

"There is a sack of glittering cannon-balls," said Ross, "which if we can carry with us, we shall not be entirely defenceless."

"Leave that to the ingenious Sneaky," said that character, capering about.

"I shall lead the expedition," Stumps announced, "because I have made this journey before the other way round. Now we shall go down the rigging instead of up it."

"Child's play," said Monkey, Tracky and Crackey, skipping up and down, "especially to midshipmen."

"We shall see, as to that," remarked poor Gravey, in his usual melancholy manner of looking on the darkest side, and remembering his narrow escape up rucksack hill.

Others remembered it too and laughed. Kings Parry and Sneaky were now standing with their arms on the sides of the canoe, pushing it gently back and forth.

"Think how it would help us, across the great rivers!" Parry said.

"It is impossible, with all my ingenuity, to move it, however," said Sneaky. "Cannon-balls, yes: the *Invincible*, no."

"Forward march, leave everything," said Bravey, clapping his arms across his chest with excitement.

"Assemble here," called Cheeky the surgeon, "you laggards, Stumps is already nearly at the top!"

Stumps was climbing the piece of string Max had left dangling from the window fastener. Max was not surprised to see this; he knew he had not moved the string.

"The thoughtful Genii Maxii," remarked the patriarch, "prepares for our every need. Up, Monkey, since you are so impatient."

Monkey swarmed up the string, followed quickly by Crackey and Tracky, singing "Way yay up she rises" as they climbed. There followed Kings Sneaky and Ross.

"Now," called Sneaky, "the bag of cannon, boys."

Sneaky had dragged Max's bag of marbles by the string round its neck to the foot of the rope. The rest now tied it on. Then it was hauled up, clinking and swaying, and landed on the sill.

"Hooray," shrilled the Twelves, above and below, as the bag was untied and the rope lowered again.

Gravey next attempted the climb and only lost his grip once.

When all the Young Men were peering down from the sill, looking like a frieze of figures in the moonlight, the patriarch was slung into a bosun's chair made by the middies, which was really a simple loop tied at the end of the string. Over his knees he held the colours. Then he was hauled up with dignified slowness, not because he could not climb, but because he was special, and was welcomed with a cheer. The sill was by now somewhat crowded with cannon-balls, the flag and Twelves.

"Untie the rope," commanded the Duke. "Foolish to leave behind what the Genii thoughtfully provide."

Of course, Max thought, as he seemed to see the string untied, and reeled tidily into a coil by willing hands. They took it with them.

They used it, he thought, even when they went down the steep creeper. And he imagined he could see Stumps heading the crawling line, followed by five more, all roped round; the rumbling bag of cannon in the middle, also tied on, then the remaining six behind. The weight of the cannon was held back by the six above, from crushing the six in front.

How sensible and brave they are, Max thought, and he seemed to hear the rustling of the leaves as they made their descent. Now and then someone slipped and cried shrilly or another scrambled, clutched and swore. But on the whole it was done in an orderly way befitting the Twelves, even to the carrying of the colours. Once at the bottom, they untied themselves, and the Duke told off four strong men to drag the cannon-balls, and they set off in a line for the front gate.

And it was here that Max's imagining became a little muddled. It was almost as if he had been left behind round the corner and could not see. But he thought he heard cries of delight and discovery, and then many of their thin voices talking together, arguing. Perhaps they were arguing which way to go. Then Butter's voice, louder and more commanding, said:

The Thoughtful Genii Maxii

"It is a carriage provided by the thoughtful Genii, it is ungrateful not to use it." Sounds of hearty agreement greeted this remark. Then Max heard a familiar kind of rumble, and saw the gleam of something which looked like a gun-carriage. The Young Men had loaded their cannon-balls on to it and, six a side, were pushing it towards the road. At the brow of the slope, he saw them clamber aboard themselves, the Duke giving a good heave and leaping on last, as a man does pushing off a boat. The small flag was held aloft in the middle.

Then with a rumble which grew fainter and fainter Max thought he saw the little chariot loaded with their crouched forms disappear down the moonlit road, towards the valley where the beck ran.

Max slept peacefully after this, without another thought.

It was only when he woke up in the morning that he thought: It was the skate! It was my skate they went on!

His mind had given him the answer while he slept.

Chapter 17

War and Peace

Max could hardly wait to tell Jane the clue of the skate, but she was down before him, having breakfast, and Mr. Morley was reading things from the paper again.

"Drat that reporter," he said. "Here's a headline—'Lost, stolen or strayed? Strange disappearance of wooden soldiers.' I told him to keep it *out* of the paper—"

"Yes, but, Dad, you have to be *nice* to them," explained Philip, "or they do it to annoy. You were beastly to him. What does it say?"

" 'What has happened to the set of old soldiers, possibly to be identified as those belonging to the Brontës, found in the attic of a farm-house recently? They have disappeared, dramatically, over-night. An American professor recently offered in the columns of this paper five thousand pounds for the Brontë soldiers.' The implication is obvious, isn't it," Mr. Morley said, frowning.

"Everyone'll think they're stolen?" Jane asked.

"And there are two more letters, one saying that there will always be wars while human nature is what it is, and why shouldn't boys play with soldiers?

" 'Boys will be boys,' he says, 'and girls will join them in such military games, whether they are Branwell Brontë and his sisters, or the children who buy lead or bright plastic soldiers today. Battle, struggle and adventure against enemies are part of the pattern of living, it seems, and much as we all now hate war, they look as if they will go on being. Until men are perfect in humanity they will fight.' " This seemed a solemn letter and there was a pause.

"Mummy, do you think people ever will be perfect in humanity, or whatever he said?" asked Jane.

"Well, do you think people could have been created with anything *less* to aim at?" she replied. "If we take it God created them."

"No, but will it be *here*, on earth?" Philip asked. "Or only afterwards, in heaven? Because I think it's dull if so, I don't know anything about heaven."

"As far as we can judge looking at history," put in Mr. Morley, "there's no sign of it happening on earth, now, is there?"

"Why not?" asked Max, fiercely. It seemed a terrible failure on the part of humanity. Why did people not do something about it?

"Because people *don't* love each other perfectly, which is what being perfect in humanity, put simply, could mean, I suppose," Mrs. Morley said. "As often as not they hate each other, and therefore they fight."

"But why does God *let* them hate each other?" demanded Max. And at once he blushed, thinking of how he had hated and fought Philip.

"That," said his father, "is the deepest and most difficult mystery we ever have to face and I don't know an answer to it. Mr. Howson will tell you it's because God gave us free will, and our will is not all good, we go wrong. Now listen, the other letter's very interesting. Shall I read it?"

"Yes," chorused the family; for it was a relief to return to the soldiers from thinking about most difficult mysteries.

" 'Sir,' he read, 'the supposition that the finding of the actual wooden soldiers, called the Twelves, loved by the Brontës, would add to our understanding of the famous family, is not so outrageous as your correspondent thinks. Let us quote what Charlotte Brontë says of them in her *History of the Year*, 1829: "I will sketch out the origin of our plays more explicitly if I can. First, *Young Men*. Papa bought Branwell some wooden soldiers at Leeds; when Papa came home it was night, and we were in bed, so next morning Branwell came to our door with a box of soldiers. Emily and I jumped out of bed, and I snatched up one and exclaimed, 'This is the Duke of Wellington! This shall be the Duke!' When I had said this Emily likewise took up one and said it should be hers;

when Anne came down she said one should be hers. Mine was the prettiest of the whole, and the tallest, and the most perfect in every part. Emily's was a grave-looking fellow, and we called him 'Gravey'. Anne's was a queer little thing, much like herself, and we called him 'Waiting-boy'; Branwell chose his and called him 'Buonaparte'." '

'Several things here are remarkable about the actual soldiers. First, Charlotte's is the perfect hero, prettiest and tallest. Is this not exactly what we should expect of the young Charlotte Brontë, the hero-worshipper, who was later to portray Mr. Rochester, the most rugged, mysterious and perfect of romantic heroes, like no man that ever was? The Duke was Charlotte's first hero amongst the Twelves, until she invented descendants of his who took his place. And note that Emily's was a grave fellow: may he not reflect Emily's own character or what Charlotte and Branwell thought of it? We are told by Branwell in *The History of the Young Men* that "Gravey's temper was still further soured by the sneers and laughter which the rest raised against him". Could his grave face have suggested to Branwell's mind the character of the melancholy, reserved, and over-serious Emily? Is it an outrageous suggestion? In Branwell's story, Emily's soldier has changed to Parry. Had Emily, in the course of their games, gone on strike against being connected with the melancholy Gravey? Perhaps she had.

"Note too that Anne's was 'much like herself . . . a queer little thing'. As for Branwell, his first admiration was for Buonaparte: Buonaparte had straddled Europe like a giant, and to the small Branwell, already full of huge dreams, the very immensity of his evil success must be fascinating. Buonaparte to the average English child was a bogey: Branwell could not help admiring him. The name of the soldier in question was later changed to 'Sneaky', which may have reflected the general feeling about Napoleon. Or did it partly reflect himself? As a character, Branwell tells us Sneaky was 'ingenious, artful, deceitful but courageous'. Branwell must have known early how to use his wiles charmingly, to get his own way. . . . Branwell shows a streak of comic realism, at times twistedly satirical, in all these young writings. For my part I should welcome the chance to make the actual acquaintance of the

Duke, of Sneaky, Gravey and Waiting-boy, probably the same soldier as Branwell calls Trott and later to become Ross. And as to the patriarch, Butter Crashey, who would not like to meet him, as it were in the flesh?"

Max listened, absorbed. All these soldiers were his friends. This man, towards whom he felt great warmth, understood, and thought of them as real. How he wished he could show them to him!

"And guess who it is? Mr. Howson!" said their father.

"Of *course*, it would be," said their mother.

"The Brontyfan," said Philip, winking at Max.

Chapter 18

The Gun-Carriage

I t was certainly crowded upon the gun-carriage. The cannon-balls themselves took up much of the room.

As the Duke gave the last push and flung himself aboard into the backs and arms and legs of Gravey, Bravey and the middies, he could not help sniffing. It was beneath his dignity, a little, to travel crammed upon a gun-carriage with the common soldier (or sailor) and he wished he were astride his good charger Copenhagen. However, escape was the main object.

"Have the goodness to move those cannon-balls and make room for my feet, Bravey," he said, clutching at Monkey to keep his balance. Bravey did so, pushing at Gravey, who heaved a deep and dismal sigh.

The wide road stretched downwards before them, clearly lighted by the moon. They had set the gun-carriage, of course, upon the crown of the road at the top of the hill, and as the wheels rumbled gently and they gathered speed, they could only trust in the Genii and hope that the road would have no sudden bends. So thought Stumps, who happened to be sitting in the front, holding on to the strap.

"I suppose you realize there is no means of steering this primitive vehicle?" he said to King Sneaky, who sat next to him.

"Leave it to the ingenious Sneaky," said this small person, who had hold of the other side of the strap. And he laughed one of his sinister laughs, as he tugged upon it. But all that happened was that Stumps's end began to rush through his hands. He tugged it back, and in this way they continued for some distance, pulling back and forth furiously. The gun-carriage kept straight on, quite unaffected.

"We can only go where the road takes us," said Butter Crashey, who stood behind them, his hand up to his eyes, gazing into the distance, "and at least we are set fair in the middle."

"If the road turns, we shall be flung into a ditch and all lost," said Gravey, "but it is no more than one can expect."

The rest jeered, and Bravey dug him with his sharp elbow, his hands being employed holding the flag.

"We cannot eat and we cannot drink," he said, trying to hop up and down on the spot, "but at least we can be merry, old fellow. Tomorrow we die."

"And the next day we are made alive," added Cheeky, his red cheeks gleaming in the moonlight. "Take heart, lads."

"I can see the sea, I can see the sea! On the right! All silver with the moon!" squealed Crackey, who was squatting on the gun-carriage, and leaning out, holding on to Ross's legs. "Up the rigging and down the plank!" he yelled. Monkey and Tracky pushed their heads about, trying to see.

"Nonsense," said the Duke sternly, looking back. "We are coming to the end of it, and you do not come to the end of the sea so quickly."

"It is a lake, no doubt," Parry remarked.

"It is darkening ahead on the right," called Ross.

"We're coming to a forest," answered Stumps, who could see the trees.

The Twelves turned to gaze into the wood, as the carriage rumbled steadily past it on the darkened road. Moonlight fell in flakes between the huge trees. Tracky seized Ross round the waist.

"Got you," he squeaked, feeling somewhat frightened. And he held on tightly. Tracky after all was only ten and it was many years since he had faced the enormous outside world.

Now they were past the dark forest, and the road stretched silver again. But what was this brilliant and gleaming golden light, in two great orbs, coming towards them so quickly they could only gasp? With the blinding shafts of light came a loud and hideous rumble.

The Gun-Carriage

"The Genii!" said Stumps, shading his eyes.

"Monsters!" hissed Sneaky.

"Turn the carriage out of the road!" yelled Monkey.

"All is lost," groaned Gravey.

The Twelves could see nothing in the approaching glare, which came rapidly closer and closer up the hill towards them.

"Young Men, down!" ordered Butter Crashey, "crouch, stoop, lower, bury your heads, it is the only chance!"

The Twelves obeyed instantly, hearing the patriarch's voice. The tall Duke had the greatest difficulty, but he somehow bent himself double. The middies folded themselves away, Stumps and Sneaky leaned forward over the front, closing their eyes, Butter himself dropped on his knees. The light became unbearably dazzling to the watching Bravey (the only man to keep his eyes open), then there was an immense roar, and total darkness enveloped them. The roar was deafening, the smell sickening, the heat of the tunnel fearful.

Then quite suddenly they were out on the other side, the lights were gone, the noise grew less, and the great lorry climbed the hill, its gears whining, and its driver unaware that he had narrowly missed squashing the Twelves and ending this tale in tragedy. Fortunately, he had not seen them, or he would have thought "Rat!" and swerved to catch it, in the cruel way of bored drivers on long night journeys.

"Tug! Pull, Stumps! Prepare to tumble, Twelves!" yelled Sneaky. "I'm going to stop this carriage somehow, for the road is too dangerous! Another monster like that, and we may be done for."

"Save your breath! One, two three, pull!" said Stumps. And together they heaved on the strap, lifted the front wheels, and succeeded in turning them a little towards the side of the road. The carriage rattled on until it met the verge, where it overturned against a tuft of grass by a rut, and flung off the Young Men, pale and breathless, but unhurt, except for Crackey who had bitten his tongue, and said so.

"You've had worse to bear," said Parry. Butter Crashey was brushing himself down. The Duke flicked dust nervously from his cuffs. Bravey planted the colours and executed a caper on the side of the road, shaking his fists at the memory of the lorry. Only Cheeky the surgeon seemed unafraid and unmoved.

"It is evident," began the patriarch, and his voice trembled slightly, "that we must now leave the main road, even if it is the shortest way home. For another time such a gigantic monster might well damage us."

"There's a cross-roads here," called Stumps, who had made haste to march along the road and explore. "A much smaller road turns off to the left. Let us take that. It's a good steep hill, and too narrow for a monster of the kind we've passed."

The Duke took command. Three a side, the Young Men pulled the carriage along by the edge of the road towards the corner. Monkey flung himself upon it, lay on his back, and bicycled with feet in the air as if he were going up the rigging, feet first. His ape-like face was still blank with fright, but this exercise made him feel better.

At the corner they stopped to consider. The main road veered right, down to the beck and the bridge. The way to the left went steeply downhill, the Genii only knew where.

"It is the exact opposite to our way home," said B. Crashey, "but instinct will guide us round. Who votes for a longer and safer journey, and who for the dangers of the high road?" The gallant Cheeky and the four kings, Parry, Ross, Sneaky and Wellington, were for risking their lives on the direct road. But they were outnumbered by the rest, who shouted them down.

They tugged the carriage to the middle of the side road, and once more packed themselves on. But their troubles were not over. Not only was the road fairly steep, so that they gathered speed quickly, it was also somewhat rutty, so that they overturned more than once in their haste. Added to this, it took several slight bends, and many were the spills at the sides before the Twelves saw looming ahead a row of cottages. Here the path turned right once more and proceeded gently always downwards.

"I scent water," said Monkey.

"I can see a river," said the Duke, looking ahead.

"It's getting light," said Bravey. "Eat, drink and be merry!"

The Gun-Carriage

"We are coming to some huge, gaunt building," remarked Ross.

It was a ruined mill. The carriage slowed down as the path ceased to slope, and the Twelves dismounted (for the last time) in the most dignified manner possible. They gathered into a subdued group and gazed up in awe at the huge, ruined building towering above them in the increasing light of dawn.

"Since it is ruined, it will no doubt be deserted," said the Duke.

"And we can safely hide here today, and march again tonight,"

added Butter. Parry and Ross agreed, and Sneaky added only a mysterious laugh, and shrugged his shoulders. Meanwhile, the three middies, all their fright forgotten, had scampered merrily off towards the river, snuffing the water. Here they found a useful footbridge, which they came back to report.

Gravey, Bravey, Cheeky and Stumps were dragging the gun-carriage, loaded now with the cannon-balls, the flag and the coil of rope, into the shelter of the ruins.

"Lend a hand, you idle fellows!" called Stumps to the midshipmen.

"Cut them open and let their blood," said Cheeky, whose duties as surgeon often led him to make such threats.

"Eat, drink, dance and be merry," sang Bravey. Gravey attended to his task and sighed.

Inside the mill, in a safe corner where they could quickly hide behind some rubble if anyone were to come, the Twelves encamped for that day. There was water in plenty from the streams round the mill, and the ingenious Sneaky even found a large silver billy-can to put it in. (It was a small empty mustard tin which some untidy child had played with and thrown down.) With three men a side, this was carried full of water to the camp corner, and they only succeeded in drenching Gravey as they put it down.

Gravey gave a melancholy howl, and the rest laughed shrilly. As for food, they had to exist on grass and cresses, but as Cheeky said, what could be healthier?

"Rum and cockles," answered Bravey at once, licking his lips.

Before the golden rise of the sun, Butter Crashey and the Duke had made a trip to the bridge. The river flowed fast and eagerly in the early light, slapping up against the stones, curling round them with bubbles and foam. A large piece of wood was borne down from beyond the mill in midstream, floating evenly and steadily. They watched until it was out of sight.

"*That* is the way to travel!" said the Duke.

"Undoubtedly," said Butter Crashey. "For this river is going back the right way. We must find or make a raft. We shall be there ten times more quickly than by tramping the edge, dragging that carriage."

They hurried back to the mill and gave the order to the Twelves to search for a boat or a raft, big enough to carry them all, their cannon-balls and their coil of rope, and for oars or paddles to direct it.

"If only we had the *Invincible*!" sighed Gravey, as he sloped off with the rest to hunt.

"Trot along," said Ross. "No time to lose, day is here," and he pinched Gravey to hurry him up.

Parry found a plank, and called the rest to help carry it. It was launched for trial on a side stream, and found seaworthy. The others brought sticks for paddles. They hid this vessel down by the stream near the footbridge, and all was ready before the first cottage door opened in the lane above them and the first twist of smoke went up faithfully into the frail blue sky. Then the Twelves climbed into their secret corner in the mill, ate their plain breakfast, and despite the persistent singing of Bravey, joined by Sneaky and Stumps, fell, one by one, asleep.

Crackey was awoken at dusk by the fearful flapping of the wings of a pigeon, coming in to roost. However, he stroked his crack to give himself courage, and woke up the rest without alarm. As soon as night came down they were on the move again, and long before moonrise, they were huddled in a hole in the river bank near their raft, waiting to embark.

"The moon rises late," said Ross, "let us not wait for it."

The patriarch put his head from the hole and gazed at the summer night. It was starry and not pitch dark.

"We will embark at once," he said. The Twelves cheered, and a water rat behind the next alder, hearing so strange a shrill sound which he did not recognize, dived into the river with a hollow plop and swam rapidly for the other shore.

The plank had this advantage, that there was a nailhole at one end, and a wide slot near the middle where another piece of wood had once been mortised to it. Monkey had passed their rope through the hole, and tied up the raft to an alder branch. Into the slot they put the bag of cannon-balls, to prevent it sliding about, planting the flag on top. When everyone else was embarked, the patriarch stepped aboard, carrying his pole over his shoulder, and made his way up to the bows. The Duke, who was the tallest, and could wield the longest pole, stood in the stern to steer, as if the raft were a punt. Then the midshipmen untied the painter, and coiled up the rope. The Duke gave a great push at the bank with his pole, and the raft was off, away into midstream and gliding gaily along over the dark twisted water, where the reflections of the stars danced.

At first nobody spoke. The Young Men waited, their hearts beating and their senses alert, for their raft to prove herself. Gravey for one expected to be flung instantly into the cold water.

But as the vessel plied her way steadily and bravely downstream, they took heart, and a contented whispering arose from amongst them.

The water-rat saw and heard these things with astonishment from the other bank.

As their eyes grew used to the dark, they could see the bushes and trees whose arms stretched over the beck. When they heard a faster tumble of water ahead, Sneaky and Stumps would call out where the rocks lay, and order the rowers on right or left to guide the raft past them by paddling. All went so well that soon the middies, joined by Bravey and Stumps, were singing a cheerful song.

"We'll rant and we'll roar, all o'er the wild ocean,
We'll rant and we'll roar, all o'er the wild seas,
Until we strike soundings in the Channel of old England,
From Ushant to Scilly is thirty-five leagues,"

they sang. And the rat, swimming along curiously behind, kept a discreet distance as he heard it.

When they had travelled what seemed to them several miles, the raft, carried swiftly by a particularly strong swirl of water round a bend in the stream, hit itself against the underpart of a large stone (which Stumps and Sneaky, being more interested in the distance between Ushant and Scilly, had failed to notice) and turned turtle sideways, sliding all but a few cautious soldiers into the water. Stumps, right in the bows, got the impact of this terrific jolt first, flew through the air, hit his head on a further stone, and when he came to, found himself in midstream, floating he knew not where in total silence and darkness.

Butter Crashey was flung against the cannon-balls which he clutched at. The Duke, Bravey and Gravey, balanced on the upside of the raft, kept their footing and righted it. The water was full of screaming, swearing, chattering Twelves. The painter was hastily untied by Bravey and flung to the less fortunate floundering in the water. The bold Cheeky rescued Crackey-aged-five, and nearly lost his own life in the process. Some scrambled on to the rock, the other two middies swam choking to the shore, Gravey

The Gun-Carriage

helped Ross and Parry aboard one by one. The patriarch came to his senses, and found he was embracing the cannon-balls and the colours. He quickly gave the order to abandon ship, for the moment, since all were too cold to sit cramped on deck. Dragging the bag of cannon-balls between them, he, Ross, and the rest still aboard, picked their dangerous way to shore by the shallow stepping stones at the side of the beck, leaping and sliding and cursing the cannon like true soldiers.

"It was Stumps's fault," said Bravey furiously, his usual good cheer gone. "Not to mention Sneaky. They were not looking where we were going." And he stuck the flag angrily in the soft earth.

"We were, we were!" screamed Sneaky.

"Old Stumpy! Bandy legs! Tump head!" went on Bravey rudely, jumping to warm himself.

"Blame none of the Twelves," said the patriarch, "only be thankful we are saved."

"I blame Tump head," repeated Bravey.

The Young Men looked about in the light of the now risen moon, expecting Stumps to answer for himself or to land Bravey a good right punch on the nose.

"Where *is* Stumps?" said several together.

The Duke and Butter began to count the men.

"Stumps, Stumps, where are you?" some called, by the river.

"He is lost," groaned Gravey, "and has paid his penalty."

The situation was too solemn for anybody to laugh.

"Nonsense," said the Duke. "Not Stumps. We shall see him again, as we always have."

"Duke of York, Frederic Guelph, Frederic the First, Frederic the Second!" called young Crackey at the river's edge, slapping his chest with his arms to warm himself.

But there was of course no answer, since Stumps was already several leagues on, and was anyway unfit for conversation.

"We will search by day," said the patriarch, "meanwhile, let us march, to warm ourselves, Wellesley."

"Certainly," said the Duke. He ordered six men to pull the cannon-balls, and Gravey to carry the rope round his neck.

" 'And but a rope to hang himself,' " sang poor Gravey, in the most quavering and melancholy of tones, which caused delight to the midshipmen in spite of the loss of Stumps.

They climbed up into the field and set out briskly downhill, the river running alongside.

Chapter 19

Butter Crashey

"So what we've got to do, Janey," Max announced when he had told her everything, "is to find my SKATE. That will give us some idea which way they've gone."

"Yes," she said. She was extremely impressed at Max's dream, or imagining, or vision, about the Young Men's departure and particularly about the string.

"And by the way, my marbles *have* disappeared," Max added. This seemed to Jane even more amazing. She opened her great blue eyes, and said, "Goodness!" very gustily.

"Come on. Let's go," Max said, leaping up.

First they bicycled to the bottom of the hill which led out of their village, down the road upon which Max thought he had imagined the Twelves going. This road took a turn to the right and went down to a beck, which they crossed by a bridge. Then it began to climb again. All the way along Jane and Max searched the verge of the road, one taking each side, for some trace, some faint clue, of the missing soldiers.

But they found nothing, not a detail which might help them, far less Max's skate. Over the bridge, when the road climbed again, Max jumped off and searched by the road.

"I thought perhaps they might have left the skate here," he said forlornly. "After all, it would be heavy to pull up hill."

"Yes," muttered Jane. It seemed hopeless. The world was so immense: the Young Men were so small.

"If only it were *snowing*, there might be the chance of tracking footsteps. They would leave footmarks, Max, tiny weeny ones, smaller than birds, like mice perhaps," Jane went on, lost in her imagination, "only not paws, shoes. In a column."

"Well, it's *not* snowing," Max said. It seemed useless to look for minute footmarks in the summer dust, or even for marks of the skate-wheels. On the road, there was nothing to mark; and as Max now pointed out, they could not use the skate except on the road, they must have a smooth surface, or it would not run.

Jane agreed.

"So where shall we go next? You know what I thought, Max, when you said this road? I thought they might be going back to Haworth. It's the direct road."

"So did I," Max admitted. Both had thought it, but neither had said it. "If not, it might be anywhere. Just to hide. Absolutely anywhere."

"Yes."

They looked gloomily over the bridge into the stream.

"We've got to try something," said Max at last, "so let's try the direct opposite. To what we thought. Take that small side road where this road turned right."

"Yes," said Jane, who, like Max, thought there was a kind of challenge to fate in taking the direct opposite.

They bicycled back up the hill and took the steeper side lane down again. They passed some cottages, and following the lane, came out at a mill.

"I say, look, it's an old mill. It's partly ruined," Jane said, "and there's the river again."

"Not the same river," Max said, "I don't suppose."

Now all round the mill it was slightly wet and marshy.

"You *might* make footprints here," Jane said. "Look, you've made some. Let's leave the bikes."

They did. They stepped gingerly, by the side of tiny puddles and cresses and shallow overflows of stream-water fringed with grass.

"You see," Max said, in a dream-like sort of tone, which Jane recognized as the one he used when he was making things up in his imagination, in their games, "you see, they camped here, for the day, it's a super place to hide."

Jane said nothing, she only looked at the muddy ground for some confirmation of what Max was saying. She could see a way into the old building, where a door was broken. It was round by the mill pond. She turned off the path and went this way. Between the pond and the door it was muddy. Jane thought she detected a two-wheel track, narrow, across this. She stooped down where it was clearest, and surely, surely those little marks beside it were the marks of their feet?

"Max!" she said sharply. "Look!"

Max looked and nodded. "Let's go in."

They pushed open the door, squeezed in, and looked round, blinking.

In the corner, by a big pile of fallen stones, gleamed Max's skate. They both exclaimed and rushed towards it and peeped behind the stones. As if the Young Men might still be there, waiting!

But there was only an old mustard tin, oval-shaped, half-full of water, and a little pile of withered water-cress.

"This is where they camped," Max said. "Look at their water!"

Jane nodded.

"And they didn't want the skate any more, so they weren't going downhill," she said.

"Or, if they were, they weren't going on a road," added Max.

"No, so they must have been going over fields?" said Jane.

"Let's go down to this river," Max said.

And he picked up his skate and went out, holding it tenderly because it was a gun-carriage which had carried the Twelves, and not merely a skate. Jane followed. They walked round the mill again and down to the stream and found the footbridge.

When Max saw the footbridge, he at once crossed it. Jane followed. Max was behaving rather as she had heard that water-diviners do, as if he were a sleep-walker. She saw no reason to stop him, since they had better look somewhere than nowhere.

The footbridge led to a footpath. Max marched along, an orchard on his left and a stone wall on his right, and the footpath led first beside the river and then away from it when the river did a bend, and then near it again, right by its brink.

And as Jane looked into it, she said, very quietly:

"You know, Max, they could have gone by river."

"I know. This way, though," Max said. "It's flowing this way."

Max scuffled along the footpath, thinking how much easier it would be for a Young Man to march here than on the grass, which to him would be quite tall. And then lying half-hidden in the grass by the path he saw the marble. Jane nearly fell over him as he bent to pounce on it. In the palm of his hand, he showed it to her.

"Recognize it?" he said. "I would, anywhere." It was a particularly translucent shade of sea-green and it had delicious wavy ripples in it, like flowing hair. Max had always privately called it the mermaid marble.

"So we're on the track," Jane said. "They've dropped it."

Max flung himself down on the grass and looked at the marble as if it were one of those crystal balls fortune-tellers have, and could tell him things. Jane sat beside him, thinking, and enjoying the sun and the noise of the water. The search for the Young Men made everything seem more magic. In every tuft of grass which the black-faced sheep had left waving uneaten, under every large weed by the path, behind every boulder, beneath every bramble or bilberry, or swinging upon a single bracken frond strayed from the moors, there might be a Young Man. How comfortably Monkey and the middies would climb that bracken stalk, crawl out on to the spread of the fern and sit there sunning themselves! How usefully they could lean, the whole lot of them, against that large puff-ball in the grass!

Max started to his feet and raced across the field to the gap in the stone wall. He was gone so fast, Jane hardly kept up with him, being still lost in her dream about the bracken. She caught Max up as he was climbing the stone step in the wall. Jane looked down at the glittering emerald moss in the wall at the bottom, and in the niche between wall and step, saw something move.

It seemed quite natural to Jane that Butter Crashey should be there, she had imagined them in so many secret places. He had stepped out of a hole where he was hiding, and now held up his arms, imploringly, his face anxious and wrinkled in case he should not be seen.

"Max!" she whispered. "Look!" And she nudged him.

As soon as the patriarch knew he had been seen, he smiled and waved and bowed his head, in relief and delight.

They slipped down on to the grass by the step, and Max picked Butter gently up. He said nothing, he was so pleased. Indeed he had some difficulty in seeing Butter clearly because his eyes had filled with tears. He had longed so much to find him again and here he was. Butter pointed to the skate in Max's other hand, and rubbed his own small hands together.

"Waiting for us," Jane whispered.

"I hoped you would find the abandoned gun-carriage, oh Genii," said Butter Crashey, "and I stationed myself in the path, for I must needs consult you. The Twelves are on their way back home."

"Do you mean to Haworth?" Max asked.

"Yes," replied the patriarch. "When I heard the fate that was likely to befall us, I knew that only there should we be safe. There, where the four Genii used to be, we shall be welcomed and cherished and no harm will come to us. Is this not so?"

Butter Crashey

"Yes, it is," Max said. It was obvious.

"They'll never let you go once you get there," Jane said.

Butter nodded, satisfied.

"So I supposed," he said. "It may take many days and we have already had two disasters." And he went on to tell them of the journey, why they had left the main road, and what had happened on the river. "And, sad to relate, oh Genii, the noble Stumps is once more lost, for which reason I implore your help." He told them where they had last seen Stumps.

"He'll be floated downstream, Butter. We will go and search for him," Max promised. "Where are the others?"

Butter Crashey stepped to the edge of Max's hand, and pointed with his minute finger to the earth.

"Underground," he whispered, smiling. "In the early dawn, we met an enormous monster, four-legged, brown, with whiskers. We opened fire at once. The cannon-balls flew fast and furious, the creature received one on its chest and right paw and leapt into the air, all four feet from the ground. As we could tell by its alarmed expression, it was far more frightened of us than we were of it, and was about to dive into its hole, when I implored it to stay."

"It was a rabbit," said Jane.

"You lost a cannon-ball," said Max, holding it up. Butter nodded.

"It proved gentle in the extreme," said Butter, "showed no wish to eat us, and led us into its domain. We have come miles in perfect safety led by this animal. I came up to watch for you, but the rest are disporting themselves in an underground hall, singing merrily, while Bravey plies them with underground water for wine. If we had but the noble Stumps, we should be happy indeed, having found the Genii."

Max had been thinking quickly.

"We will search for Stumps. When will you march again?" he said.

"Tonight," said Butter Crashey.

"We shall come and watch over you," Max said. "We will go now and work out the way, and at the same time look for Stumps."

Butter bowed his thanks and smiled. Jane and Max smiled back, gravely.

"Good-bye, noble Crashey," Max said putting him down.

"Until tonight," said Jane.

The patriarch hurried along by the wall, turned off at a knot of grass, and dived underground.

Chapter 20

The Brave
Old Duke of York

As Stumps floated along on his back, what had seemed the total silence of his swoon changed to a gentle, swirling jingle, the song of the river. And what had seemed total darkness became a bewildering pattern of black branches and moving leaves and moon fall and swinging stars. And the stars were not those which had shot and exploded in his poor head when he banged it, but natural, friendly stars winking above him in the heavens.

Then Stumps knew that he was alive, and had no need even of Cheeky's ministrations to make him so.

"Huzzah, I'm not done for yet," he said to himself, "but I had better see where I am going."

So he turned himself over on to his front, and instead of floating helplessly, which his partly wooden constitution had made possible, began to swim. He also began to sing "Lillabullero" in his well-known courageous way, until a mouthful of foaming water put an end to the song and very nearly to Stumps. He choked, coughed, and grabbed breathlessly at a black shape he thought was a stone, only to find it sleek and soft and moving.

It was that inquisitive rat. He had followed the floating Stumps downstream, less afraid of him than of the eleven screaming Young Men in the water, and determined to find out what they were.

Stumps at once thought "Crocodile!", being used to Africa. "Now I am done for!" And the shock brought him fast to his senses and he struck out for a flat stone. The crocodile followed, but far from grabbing his leg as he scrambled up the stone, he nosed gently at him, his whiskers pointed forward and his eyes shining.

"What ARE you?" he said at last, in some exasperation.

"I am Frederic Guelph, Duke of York, and sometime King of the Twelves, otherwise known as Stumps," said that Young Man, controlling the chatter of his teeth with difficulty. "And what are you?" he added, determined to give as good as he got.

"A water-rat," said the other.

Stumps breathed more easily.

"Where does this river go?"

"I nobbut know t' stretch down to t' brig below here, where it meets t' other beck. I'm bound for t' brig me-sen. Tha can have a ride if tha likes to jump up."

This is an extremely polite animal, thought Stumps, and it is better to get to the bridge, where I can wait for the rest, than to be stranded on a stone in midstream, or hurtled along further than I want to go. So he bowed, and said he would be obliged, and

mounted the rat's neck. He was borne comfortably down the river, able to look about him.

"Did you happen to notice what befell my companions?" he asked nonchalantly.

"I think all t' lot on 'em got ashore," replied the rat.

"Excellent," said Stumps. "No more than I should expect."

"Are you foreigners in these parts?" asked the rat.

"On the contrary," Stumps replied, "we have been hereabouts for well over a hundred years. And our patriarch was in fact one hundred and forty when he began: so I leave it to you to calculate his years now."

"I haven't oft known onnybody *start* at a hundred and forty," the rat remarked: and became so involved in mental arithmetic that he barely noticed the bridge.

It loomed above Stumps, a wide and noble curve in the moonlight. The rat landed him upon a stone, whence he could easily walk to the shore, and then disappeared himself into a hole in the other bank. Stumps watched the happy water for a little, then found himself a hidden place on the bank and fell asleep.

It was high noon when he awoke, and he was awoken by voices. The sun shone through the arbour of leaves behind which he sat and warmed his shoulder deliciously. The voices were familiar, and though monstrously loud they were not frightening to Stumps because he half-recognized them.

"This'll be the way, Janey," called Max. "I bet this road leads round to Haworth."

"Yes, you can see it will. It's miles for them to go, but they'll cross this bridge. We'll go back and get our bikes in a tick and bicycle right round," answered Jane.

"I say, Jane, what a super place to play! Look at all these marvellous stepping-stones. And under the bridge there'll be tiddlers! And boats! It's terrific for boats. I know, let's go and get the Ashanti canoe!"

It was the Genii. Stumps had scrambled to his feet, rubbing his eyes, realizing only this, that he must make himself quickly obvious. *They* could rescue him, they could tell him where the others were, they, particularly Max, were his protectors. He parted the leaves, ran from his hole, scrambled down the bank, and on to the first stone. The voices had stopped, where were they? "Oh Genii," Stumps said, "here I am, notice me."

He could hear footsteps, above him, on the bridge.

"Come on, we shan't be long."

"All right, what a marvellous idea!"

Stumps scrambled and leapt from stone to stone, his thin arms balancing him. Then he looked up at the bridge, waved his arms, danced, even tried a small, thin shout.

He heard only a commotion in the trees by the beck, and the sound of footsteps, running.

Stumps stood gazing at the bridge and gulped. He was so small compared with them, they had not seen him, they did not care, even, perhaps.

But here Stumps pulled himself up. He was quite sure the Genii Maxii cared. What about the adventure of the creeper? He flicked away minute tears, and said: Come back, Genii, I am here.

Perhaps this was why Jane stopped breathless on the footpath, when they were nearly back at the mill.

"Max," she said in tones of horror. "We're supposed to be looking for Stumps, we've forgotten Stumps, how could we, we promised!"

Max went scarlet and then white.

"Help. It was that canoe idea. Shall I go back?"

"What about the bikes? We can't bring them this way, over all these walls, really, can we?"

"No. We'll have to bike back home, get the canoe, and go round by the road the other way to the bridge. Come on, hurry. Poor Stumps: I've been looking all the way along, in the river. I didn't forget for long," Max said, guiltily.

Stumps sat down upon his stone and waited for what seemed to him hours and hours. The sun had warmed the stone and made it very comfortable. He wondered where the others were, and whether Crashey had yet sent out search parties. Would it be better if he followed this river back the way he had come, hoping to find them? This was what he would do if the Genii did not return.

But the Genii did return. Stump's heart leapt for joy as he heard their voices once more. They jumped off their bicycles. The Genii Maxii came scrambling down the bank, quite near him.

"I'm going to search every hole and every stone along this bank," he shouted.

"I thought we were going to launch the canoe," said the Genii Janeii, following him and doing so.

"You can. I must look for Stumps," Max said, sounding worried and ashamed. "He could have been washed ashore anywhere."

Stumps almost laughed. They had even brought the *Invincible* to rescue him. It only remained to attract their great attention and avoid the Genii Janeii's large, pink, bare feet, as they tiptoed from stone to stone.

"It's floating beautifully. There's a frog on that stone. It's going to jump. See?"

"Where?" Max hurried across. Stumps waved his arms and shouted with all his might. "That's not a frog, that's Stumps!" shrieked Max. "Careful, Jane, bring the boat alongside, he can get in, he'll like it! Oh, Stumps, where have you been?" Max whispered, stooping down.

Stumps flung himself lightly over the edge of the canoe, and turned to smile at them. He felt much relieved. So did they.

"I've had a good idea," said Max, when Stumps had disported himself in the *Invincible*, making several journeys with the Genii in command. "We'll leave it down here. Ready. It may be useful. For tonight. And we'll find some sticks for paddles."

"We must hide it, though, it's precious," Jane said.

They did this, to their satisfaction, and then Max picked up Stumps. They hurried back along the footpath, and Stumps sang "Marlbrook s'en va-t'en guerre" all the way along in a voice like a gnat, but it jerked as Max moved. It reminded Jane of singing as her mother dried her hair, when she was little.

When they reached the stone step and the burrow, they knelt down.

"Now, Stumps, Frederic I and II," said Max, "announce yourself. The patriarch and the rest are hidden underground. Tell them to make their way tonight to the bridge. You can guide them."

Stumps nodded and marched boldly into the hole, calling in a loud voice, "Crashey! Crashey!"

The call grew fainter and fainter. Then Jane and Max, with their ears to the ground, thought they could hear a shrill, distant cheer, as the Young Men welcomed Stumps, and the sound of many voices chanting the old chant, "Stumps! Stumps! Here is Stumps!"

"That's all right," Max said.

That night they made careful plans. Jane looked up moonrise in her diary, borrowed an old alarm clock of Philip's, and set it for half an hour before.

The alarm clock woke Philip, as well as Jane. Not only this, he had already wondered why Janey wanted to get up early and needed waking on a summer morning. When he realized it was the middle of the night, he was suspicious. He sat up in bed, and heard stealthy movements from Jane's room next door. Philip had already noticed that Max and Jane suddenly seemed far less worried and sad about the loss of the wooden soldiers than they had appeared at first. Added to this, when their father or mother spoke of them, and wondered where they were, and if they would ever hear of them again, Max and Jane looked what Philip called "cagey". Trying very hard to look non-committal, they succeeded in looking conscious. He had already wondered if Max and Jane knew where the soldiers were, and were not telling. For Mr. Morley had been persuaded not to go to the police. Meanwhile Mrs. Morley had told Philip he should cable the American professor tomorrow, to say they were lost, and prevent his fruitless errand. Philip was loth to do it, and kept hoping that the soldiers would be heard of.

So it was no wonder that Philip connected this strange nocturnal behaviour of Jane's with the disappearance of the soldiers.

He heard Jane tiptoe down, and Max follow her.

He leapt out of bed and looked out of his window. His room, unlike Max's, faced the front. A half-moon lay floating on her back like an idle silver cradle, and the billows of lapping cloud seemed to make her rock. He heard them bringing their bikes round from the yard. Wheeling them stealthily on the grass verge, they went out of the front gate and set off down the hill. If he did not hurry he would lose them. He flung on slippers and topcoat, fled downstairs, seized his own bike and followed.

Philip spun down the hill feeling an excitement like a bubbled wine. He could just see their bicycle lamps ahead in the distance as the road turned right. The moon spread a silver icing over the reservoir which Crackey had thought was the sea. The wood by the road was as dark as enchantment. He sped after Max and Jane.

Now they were crossing the road bridge over the beck, and he could see the water, silvered. This was the direct road to Haworth. Philip kept his distance, he would rather not be seen. Before the houses of Haworth began, they took a sharp turn on the left, downhill. Now, if he was unlucky, they would see his lamp, should they chance to look back along the main road.

Philip knew where this lane led, he had already thoroughly explored their new surroundings. It led, once, through a farm-gate, along a stony track to the old packhorse bridge. He would have to be careful now or they would hear him, on the stony lane behind them.

When he reached the bridge and saw their bicycles stacked, he decided to stay there. They must be coming back. He leaned over the bridge and gazed at the water. Then he saw the bicycle lamps, casting small searchlights all round the other end of the bridge, down each bank, over the stones, and the water, into the overhanging bushes and holes.

Max and Jane were searching for something. Philip heard them whisper (always, at night, one seems to whisper: why is it so?) and saw the bike lamps going away over a field path, the other side of the bridge.

"I thought they'd be here already," Jane said.

"So did I. Mind where we walk, Jane," answered Max. "I expect they'll keep to the footpath, don't you?"

But when they reached the stone wall and step and the rabbit hole, and still had not met the Young Men, they were worried.

"We've missed them. We ought to have said an exact place."

"We said the bridge. It doesn't matter so long as they're safe. Only I'd like to see them over the beck."

"So would I."

They flashed the lamps right and left.

Jane said: "They'd come out, if they were here, they'd see our lamps. Let's wait. They may have come a roundabout way." She sat down on the field-path not far from the bridge and Max flopped beside her.

"Isn't it fun being out at night?" she said.

"I'd be afraid if you weren't here," Max admitted.

"So would I, a bit, if you weren't," said Jane.

She lay back and looked at the moon, and suddenly sat up again as if she had lain on a thistle.

"Maxy! Listen!" she said, putting her ear to the ground.

Beneath the cold grass they could hear the faint and distant strains of martial music. Their ears to the ground, they listened, hardly breathing. The sound became clearer and clearer until it was recognizable. Frail, insect-like singing, but singing, a marching song sung to a brisk measure. Now Max could hear the words, though still muffled.

> *"Oh the brave old Duke of York,*
> *He had ten thousand men;*
> *He marched them up to the top of the hill,*
> *And he marched them down again."*

Then the song emerged, clear and fast like an underground beck reaching the surface. Max and Jane stood up and looked about them. Just ahead, from another hole, came the column of the Young Men, two by two, singing lustily.

> *"'And when they were up, they were up,*
> *And when they were down, they were down,*
> *And when they were only half-way up,*
> *They were neither up nor down,"*

they sang.

Crackey and Tracky, first, now clapped hands for several paces to the rhythm, having no drum at hand. Monkey and Cheeky. Gravey and Bravey with the flag. Parry and Ross and the cannon-balls. Sneaky and Stumps. The Duke and the patriarch. Jane kept them in the beam of her lamp, while Max turned his discreetly away.

The sight was so enchanted that Max and Jane said nothing, but watched the march of the Twelves from behind until they reached the approaches to the bridge.

"They'll expect us there, if Stumps gave the message," Max whispered.

Jane nodded.

Max came up gently as the Twelves halted, turned off his lamp, and stooped down.

"It is I, the Genii, oh Twelves," he whispered.

They cheered.

"Will you cross by land or by water?" Max said. "The canoe is moored at the edge."

The Twelves were tired after their long underground march and chose water. Moreover, despite their adventure last night, they had an irresistible tendency to choose water. They had never forgotten the *Invincible* and the journey to Africa.

Philip, cold on the bridge, at last saw Jane's bike lamp lighting up the far bank and the flat stones. He saw Max crouching down over the water. He thought he saw them launching the Ashanti canoe. Philip now turned on his own strong lamp, shone it down upon the water, and saw the strangest sight he had ever seen.

Caught in the beam, the canoe began to cross the black water, ferried by small, sensible, active, wooden soldiers, using poles and paddles of stick, shouting orders to each other, rounding the stones with care, and at last safely drawing towards the near bank.

Max and Jane thudded past him on the bridge.

"Phil!" gasped Jane, as she ran past. Philip felt sick in his stomach.

Chapter 21

What Are
Genii For?

"Maxy!" Jane whispered urgently, catching him up, "did you see, Phil's followed us!"

"I know," said Max quietly. "I can't help it, we've got to get them safely ashore." Max picked his way down the steep bank, and was ready to grasp the bows of the canoe as it glided to shore. It was still held in the beam of Philip's torch. The patriarch held both arms in the air, and Max could see he was smiling.

"The Genii are everywhere," he said. One by one the Young

What Are Genii For?

Men disembarked as Max held the boat, and began climbing the bank of the river like General Wolfe's men up the Heights of Abraham. Some went on all fours, some clung to stalks and grasses, one suggested using the rope which still hung round Gravey's neck, but the rest were too impatient to wait. Gravey himself stumbled more than once, lost his footing and rolled back upon the Duke. As for Ross, he was attempting to haul the bag of cannon-balls, the rest having forgotten them in their haste. Added to this the beam of light was momentarily gone, and the moon did not reach the dark bank under the side of the bridge.

Max turned on his own lamp, and relieved Ross of the marbles. Butter Crashey came last as usual, in his alert and dignified manner, though even he had to scramble in places.

At the top of the bank waited Jane, who was now shining her lamp to guide them. And Philip.

Philip was squatting down, holding his own lamp steady, as if to see better what he could not believe. He was perfectly quiet, and rather pale. He watched the mountaineering of the Twelves with growing excitement and the whole mystery of Max's behaviour made itself clear as he watched. He felt sharp regret and jealousy that he had not known sooner. But Jane's gentle quietness as she had whispered, "Hullo!" prevented his bursting out with, "Why didn't you TELL me?" as he wanted to. He realized that his presence might frighten them, his voice would be unknown. Why had he not seen they were alive when he handled them in the attic? He supposed they feigned wooden when they chose. Philip was not stupid. He fitted the pieces neatly into the puzzle as he crouched there watching.

Now they were forming themselves into a column, two by two, on the road. This strange, squeaking, crackling noise! It must be their voices. Could Jane and Max understand what they said? If so, it only needed practice. He strained his ears, concentrating.

Max scrambled up the bank, last, saw Philip, took in the look on his face, and reached an immediate decision. He stooped down to the patriarch.

"The third Genii is here, oh Patriarch," Max said clearly, picking Butter up, "will you meet him?"

What Are Genii For?

Butter Crashey blinked in the strong light of the bike lamp, and nodded.

Max held the small soldier out to Philip between his finger and thumb. "Gently," he whispered. "Butter Crashey."

Philip put out his hand, almost gingerly. Max placed Butter upon it.

"This is the Genii Philippi," said Max.

Philip was reminded of the ghost of Julius Caesar, but he did not smile. The little creature was speaking. He bent his head. Then, afraid of tipping him off, he dared to pick him up in finger and thumb and put him to his ear. He was warm and soft. Alive.

"The Twelves welcome you," said Butter Crashey; and this time, Philip made out the words. "I am their patriarch."

"I am proud to make your acquaintance, oh Butter Crashey," said the Genii Philippi, solemnly, taking Max's tone. Butter bowed and waved his arms and smiled. Jane loved to see him smile. Max sighed with relief. Philip handed the patriarch to him, still looking as dazed as if he expected to wake up and find this a dream.

"Keep straight up this narrow track, Butter Crashey, until you reach a farmyard. There you can camp tomorrow. We shall find you a place." And Max put the patriarch down, heard the Duke call attention, and saw the Twelves ready themselves.

The three Genii watched, then, as the brave column set off once more along the rough sunken lane, in the moonlight. Philip looked after them. What was it like? Like some loosely articulated lizard, or huge version of a centipede, by the road. But no, it was like nothing he had ever seen, that small column moving steadily, throwing its separate shadows, the little paper flag held above it.

"They're marching to Haworth," Max said at last.

"Yes," said Philip. And he sounded shy. Jane could understand this: he was confounded by what he saw.

"Will you write and put off that professor?" said Max anxiously.

"Yes," said Philip, "tomorrow. Well, Monday."

"No one else knows," said Jane softly.

"I won't tell," said the Genii Philippi. "But what happens when they get there? Everyone'll see them."

What Are Genii For?

"We don't know," said the others. "We can't imagine."

"And I don't know how to get them inside the museum without anyone seeing. You see they hate being picked up and organized, they like to do it themselves," Max explained.

"I haven't thought as far as that," said Jane, "what with first losing them all and then Stumps again."

"I'll help you think of a way," said the Genii Philippi. "Hadn't we better go after them?"

Weary and footsore, the slowly moving column of the Twelves tramped up the long hill, held in the three beams from the Genii's bike lamps. The moon was often hidden behind clouds, and high walls hedged them in. Their way would have been dark indeed had the Genii not been like a pillar of fire behind them. So Philip whispered, shivering. Max had the canoe balanced upon his bike basket. Jane, feeling hungry herself, was worrying about the Twelves' hunger. The Twelves, like well-disciplined soldiers, sang to keep themselves going.

They reached the farm yard before dawn. Philip knew the layout. He led the Young Men over to a small straw-stack, where between the balanced bales they could sleep warm and hidden. The little cave of straw looked cosy and inviting as he shone his lamp into it. The Twelves filed in, singing.

"Be careful tomorrow, Butter Crashey, don't come out in the daylight without looking, people will be about in the fields," whispered Max.

"I shall do all you say," replied the patriarch, and he disappeared into the straw.

The Genii bicycled home, cold, tired and a little grumpy. They said hardly a word, and Philip least of all. But their hunger was such that they one and all raided the larder, and as they stood in the kitchen munching, Jane said in a whisper:

"They'll be so *hungry*. I must take them something tomorrow."

"Oh, they'll forage," said Philip, as he tiptoed off to bed. "Soldiers always do."

Philip was right. This was exactly what next morning the Young Men decided they must do.

It was all very well at first, as they flopped down comfortably in

148

the warm soft straw, so tired with the march that they thought of nothing but sleep. "Better than the captain's cabin," muttered Monkey, climbing up on to a bale of his own.

"Capital quarters and no mistake," said the Duke. "Fodder for horses, too." And he yawned hugely.

"The elder Genii knows what he is about," remarked Sneaky. "He is as artful and ingenious as . . . as. . . ."

"The ingenious Sneaky," muttered Parry. "You make the Genii in your own image."

"Hush," growled Gravey, "can we not sleep and be thankful?"

"Bless my liver and lights," said Bravey, "if that Gravey doesn't still whine! Give us good cheer, man!" And he planted the flag in the straw and curled up beneath it.

Crackey and Tracky were already snoring, their young legs were so tired. Ross had found himself a good nest and would not bother to talk. The stout-hearted Cheeky, leaning against Stumps, drew a long sigh of contentment, which shuddered through Stumps like a wind in the rigging. Stumps moved up, and curled into a ball on his own.

The patriarch surveyed what he could see of the noble Twelves, by the light of the moon which now happened to shine into the chink, but this was precious little. He could, however, *hear* them, snoring, sighing, grunting or muttering according to temperament, and secure in the feeling that they were all safe, fell asleep himself.

This was all very well.

But what of the sharp pangs of hunger which assailed them at daybreak? What was this that gnawed at Stumps as he sat up, clasping his stomach? Crackey was already crawling round the cave, searching diligently for grains left in the straw; but no grains are left by a harvester, he found not a single one, and was reduced to chewing a stalk.

"Hunger gnaws me vitals," said Bravey.

"Abstinence is all very fine," replied Cheeky the surgeon, now waking up, "but starvation is known to be bad for the system."

"Speeches, speeches," said Parry. "Let us go and forage."

"An army marches on its stomach," said the Duke wisely. "We must stoke up, or we shall run down."

What Are Genii For?

"Only a few green herbs in that animal's cellar," said Gravey dolefully.

"You were glad enough of them," Ross argued, jabbing him with a sharp elbow.

"I did not so much as have that," Stumps remarked stoically, "since you had eaten them all. I'm going outside."

"Stop, halt," said the patriarch, who had listened to these complaints (like those of the Israelites in the wilderness) with increasing anxiety. "I was particularly warned by the Genii Maxii to take care, monsters will be about. I forbid any Young Man to go outside until I have reconnoitred. I may myself find food enough, manna in the wilderness, who knows." He looked round the cave, now lit up by a pencil of sunlight through the crack.

"Empty me that cannon-ball bag, Ross," he ordered. For Max had decided to leave them their cannon. Ross did so. Taking the sack over his shoulder, the patriarch stepped cautiously out. He blinked in the sunlight and looked about him. He found he was facing a green close-cropped field upon which a vast number of immense, white birds walked, pecking viciously and clucking in stupid pleasure. He could see they were birds, for they sometimes flapped their great wings. What were they pecking? If it were grain, then it exactly suited his purpose. He did not want to invite a peck upon his rear portions from one of those sharp beaks, but he thought he could pick his way gently and not be seen. He saw no people, only the flock of chickens.

He set forward over the grass, eagerly. Wide drifts of seed! Scattered bountifully on the earth! Like the manna for grumbling Israel! B. Crashey stooped at a convenient drift and began to shovel it into the mouth of his sack with his tiny hands. He knelt to his task, for his back ached, one hundred and forty plus as he was. He moved on over the field, gathering the food for his men. Ahead was a building, but it seemed deserted, and it was far off. Daintily avoiding the fowls and dragging the increasingly heavy sack, Butter gleaned the seed, becoming careless in his zeal to collect more. The Twelves, who had come to the door of their refuge, watched in glee, and Cheeky was begging the Duke to order a forage party to help drag the sack.

What Are Genii For?

Suddenly from behind the chicken house bounced a huge black and white monster on all fours, and following him a man. They strode towards the stooping Butter Crashey, the dog making feints to bounce at the chickens, who pretended to flee, and squawked loudly.

The dog saw the small thing moving in the grass, and pounced, sniffing. The farmer saw the bright cotton bag. Butter seized the sack, and turned in each direction, tugging it with him. Then he felt the slobber of the animal and its hot breath and rough tongue, and at once feigned dead and kept still.

The dog snuffled. The farmer stooped idly down, curious about the bag.

It warn't a mouse, as he had thought. Why, whatever was it? A wooden soldier . . . nay!

He lifted Butter aloft and stared. Old fashioned, well made, a bit shabby, like: not a bit like new 'uns. And a lile cotton poke gain-hand it, full of his hens' corn. It were a caution! Or nobbut a bit of bairns' laiking, left ovver from yesterday? Aye, why, mebbe some of them bairns from t' cottages.

He looked at Butter again and noted his high hat. Now then, what about all this talk of ancient wooden soldiers? There'd been a piece about 'em in t' paper, think on. Hadn't he read that they'd all disappeared? Mebbe this was one on 'em; but, if so, what had gotten all t' rest?

Happen he could get on to t' paper office tonight: they'd likely be oppen, doing Monday's issue.

He picked up the bag of corn. Nobbut half full. Funny. He could have sworn he'd seen t' lile chap move, wick as owt—aye, and t' poke and all. He mun be getting daft. . . . Nay, but why had t'dog pounced? Rover'd thowt it were a mouse and all, choose what!

The horrified and hungry Twelves, watching from their stack, saw their patriarch stuffed ignominiously, head first, into the monster's pocket, and the food he had so laboriously gathered shaken out once more to the undeserving hens. The bag was dropped, empty, on the ground.

As for the noble patriarch, he unfroze to find himself lying on

What Are Genii For?

his face in a dark, smelly, prickly hammock along with a coil of rope, which he hoped was not an evil omen, a large pointed stake almost as big as himself, and what appeared to be a crumpled, dirty sheet.

Butter made up his mind to do all he could to escape from these unattractive bed-fellows, but he was quite aware that for the moment he must remain frozen when the monster touched him.

At breakfast the farmer remembered the soldier, and pulling him out of his pocket from amongst the string, the nail and the handkerchief, stood him on the table to show his family. Butter Crashey was passed from hand to hand, often head first or upon his back, and at least once he was dropped. But he took all patiently. He was also discussed as if he were not there and once more heard the tale of the five thousand pounds and the fearful threat from America. His benign expression did not alter, and indeed it was noticed by a small boy of about Max's age. More than ever was Crashey glad that they had decided to march to Haworth, and more than ever was he determined to escape.

But when he found himself standing high up on a mantelshelf, far from his friends, hungry and assailed with memories of delicious chicken seed, one thought only was left to comfort him.

This was that the rest would surely tell the Genii of his plight (for he knew they had watched him from the stack, he had seen them). And if the chief Genii, and the older Genii, and the gentle Genii could not effect his rescue, then what were Genii for?

Butter sighed deeply and let himself freeze.

Chapter 22

Wooden Soldiers
Going to Haworth

The Genii Philippi spent most of Sunday demanding a full and detailed account of the Young Men's doings from his brother and sister. All three of them were sleepy in the afternoon and they lay in the sun in the garden while Max and Jane recounted and Philip kept asking questions and could not help a few reproaches. "If only I'd seen that," he sighed. Or, "I should have done this, given them that, or the next thing," he suggested, showing an ingenuity worthy of Sneaky himself. And he had fetched his mother's book and looked up all their names once more and made Max describe their characters and sayings.

How to drag themselves out of bed again that night, they hardly knew, but like faithful Genii they did not falter in their duty. They presented themselves at the straw-stack just after moonrise, wondering if the Twelves would have gone, only to find a dejected eleven, still waiting hopelessly for their patriarch, and to hear the terrible tale of Butter Crashey's capture. Added to the woe of losing him was the Young Men's fear that without their oracle, they would not be able to get in touch with the Genii, so they cheered wanly at the sight of them.

Philip and Max decided at once that they must march, and march quickly, in case the patriarch should be recognized for what he was, an antique soldier, and in case the fame of the Brontë soldiers should cause the farmer to search in his straw and round his land for the rest. Meanwhile the thoughtful Jane fed them. She had brought crumbs and sugar and wild strawberries and milk, and the starving Twelves fell upon these like locusts. (For they had only essayed a few hasty rushes for chicken seed, and that when the greedy chickens had had most of it.) Bravey even began to sing "Cannikin clink" as he seized the acorn cup she had brought and took his turn at the milk. But finding it a feeding rather than an intoxicating fluid, he made a face and swigged it down for duty. Their spirits rose after their meal and when they set out several of the Twelves sported small, curled, white chicken feathers in their hats, like tiny, ostrich plumes.

The Genii oversaw their night's march, with the Duke in charge, and left them encamped near dawn in a field off the footpath, in the shelter of a rustling forest of oats. It was warm, hidden, and would provide food. They promised to do all they could to get back the noble patriarch. And Max, deciding that the loose cannon-balls would hinder their progress, now took charge of his marbles.

As they picked up their bikes again from the nearest point on the road, Philip looked back towards Haworth.

"They'll do it in another night," he said.

"That's what I thought," said Max.

"We'll have to get it all taped tomorrow."

"Poor *Butter*," sighed Jane, as they spun along. It had begun to rain. This time they had had the foresight to put some food in their own rooms, and tumbling straight into bed, Max munched his under the covers, swept out the prickly crumbs, and fell asleep feeling happy in spite of the fate of poor Crashey. Why was this? It was because of the Genii Philippi, whose added years and powers would help them to plan the last important part of the journey of the Young Men.

After breakfast the next day, Philip went to the post office and sent the cable, as he had promised. It cost a good deal of his pocket money and it did cross his mind to wonder whether the other Genii would share this expense and pay him back; but then he realized that it was his own fault, and stifled his meaner instincts under a necessary generosity.

"Wooden Soldiers going to Haworth," he cabled, to Professor Seneca D. Brewer. There was still time for it to reach him before he flew on the fifteenth. He wondered if he should say Regret wooden soldiers . . . or put Sorry on the end. But in the first place he did not regret it, it was obvious that Haworth was their place:

and in the second he could not afford an extra word. He would write him a letter, but of course he would not tell him the real reason.

He bicycled home to the others, feeling relieved. It had not once occurred to Philip to regret, either, the five thousand pounds which might have been Max's, so much more important had the troop of living little men become to him than the sum of money.

"If they'd only told me earlier, the silly asses, I'd have understood," he said for the hundredth time. He found the others waiting for him and reported what he had done.

"Thank goodness," Max said, glad that this threat at least was over. "But look, Phil, look at this, that we've just found, in the paper!"

And Max pointed out to Philip a small paragraph tucked away in a corner on an unimportant page, which he and Jane had spotted.

" 'Missing Soldier Found?'," read Philip, looking at the heading. "Gosh," he put in. "He hasn't wasted much time!" And he went on reading. " 'Walking over his land early on Sunday morning, a farmer near Haworth found a wooden soldier of early nineteenth-century design. He at once conjectured that this might be one of the soldiers found recently at a nearby farm, which disappeared mysteriously from there one day last week. No report of their having been found has yet been received, but does this perhaps give a clue to their whereabouts? An American professor recently offered five thousand pounds for the set of soldiers once owned by the Brontës as children. The soldiers found at the farm were reported to be of the right period and design. Where are the rest of them hiding?' "

Philip looked up at the others. If he had known, he said, how to gnash his teeth, he would have gnashed them.

"That'll be our reporter then. This person who found Butter must have rung up the paper! On Sunday, too! It's a good thing we made them march on, Max."

"Yes. But what about Butter?" said Max.

"You see the five thousand offer still stands, for all anyone knows. He's probably thinking of that, this farmer."

Wooden Soldiers Going to Haworth

"Anyway, everyone round here's interested. Bill asked me the other day if we'd found them and I had to hedge," Jane said.

"If it gets out about the professor not coming," Philip said, thinking, "then everyone will know *we* know where they are."

The others looked at him.

"You see, I cabled *Wooden soldiers going to Haworth*," Philip added. There was silence.

"Well, never mind," Max said anxiously, "they'll be there, tonight!"

Jane nodded, "Then they'll be safe. If only we can get Butter back!"

"Yes and if we can get them safely IN," Max said questioningly to Philip, his face creased up with thinking about this problem. "I think we'll just have to go the next morning and smuggle them in. Camp them in the garden, when they arrive, and tell them to wait?"

"No, I've got a better idea than that," Philip said. "Listen."

Philip's plan was bold and desperate, but if it worked it would enable the noble Young Men to re-enter their original home with the kind of dignity which befitted them, and completely, as Phil said, under their own steam. This was very important to Max, for he had quite early realized that part of their life depended on their being left to do things by themselves and not being interfered with. He could oversee and suggest, but not dictate. And they had undertaken the whole march without consulting him.

"I wonder, I just wonder," Jane said, "if when they get there, and the people find them, and the visitors all come and stare at them, if they'll freeze?"

"Not all the time," Max said. "Think of people's faces, if they see them move!"

"You know, I'm afraid," Philip said cautiously, "Jane may be right." Max's face went blank.

"It'll be beastly if so, I shall wish I'd never let them go," he said.

" 'Let them go,' " echoed Jane. "You know you wouldn't stop them, you keep on about their having to do what they think! I'm sure it's right, whatever happens afterwards."

Wooden Soldiers Going to Haworth

Max nodded dolefully.

"Yes, only I shall miss them," he said.

Philip's plan also demanded that they visit the museum at Haworth to see the lie of the land. This they arranged without further ado. Mrs. Morley was pleased to think they were keen enough to do this on their own and presented them with their shillings. So much the better, Phil said, as they jumped on their bicycles. They had decided that for the moment they could do nothing about Butter Crashey; they knew, after all, where he was. Later, perhaps they would go and ask for him.

As they entered the grey-stone, creepered parsonage, each was thinking different thoughts. Max's mind was mainly upon what his mother had told him of the Chief Genius Brannii the other day. Max was particularly interested in Brannii, since he considered himself the chief of the present Genii. So his mother had told him all she could remember about Branwell, how funny and gay and brave his early stories were (for there were lots more beside *The History of the Young Men*) and how sad it was that he disappointed everyone by never properly using the gifts he had when he grew up. His nervous, excitable, feeling temperament and his over-sheltered childhood made it difficult for him ever to grow up at all. In some ways he never did. Also his adoring family expected too much of him too early, and the more he failed, the more despairing he grew, and the more he drowned his disappointment in himself in drink at the "Black Bull" and drugs from the chemist.

He had died at only thirty-one years old, not knowing about his famous sisters' success with their novels. But what Max was thinking of, as he marched up the seven stone steps to the door, was Charlotte's comic description of him, "a low slightly built man attired in a black coat and raven grey trousers, his hat placed nearly at the back of his head, revealing a bush of carroty hair so arranged that at the sides it projected almost like two spread hands, a pair of spectacles placed across a prominent Roman nose. . . ." He had a black neckerchief and a little black cane flourished in his hand, and he walked "with that indescribable swing always assumed by those who pride themselves on being good pedestrians". And it seemed to Max that he could almost imagine him bounding down the stone staircase to the hall, to set out upon some walk over the moors. He was not at all surprised that he had invented and made alive the adventurous swashbuckling Twelves, Stumps and Sneaky and the rest, the lovable Butter Crashey, the wild uproarious middies.

But Jane was thinking of Charlotte, and wondering which room she had sat in to write *Jane Eyre* and whether she thought of herself as Jane, and if her husband Mr. Nicholls were at all like Mr. Rochester.

And Philip was surveying the outside of the parsonage, its walls and windows, and deciding exactly how his plan was to be carried out.

They explored everywhere. Jane loved the kitchen with the bright copper pans, and was stricken silent to see Charlotte's dresses with their tiny, tiny waists. Philip went quickly round, seeing the layout of the house inside, before he looked at any of the exhibits. And Max—when Max found amongst the tiny books they had written, in the minute, neat, black writing done to look like print, one which said *Second Series of the Young Men's Magazines,* he gasped, and clutched Jane's arm, and together they read the title page out in a whisper.

"They even wrote magazines for them!" Max said.

"No wonder they talk so cleverly!" Jane answered.

"Janey, they really ought to be put with their magazines," suggested Max.

But Philip decided the nursery was the place, the little narrow room at the head of the stairs in the front of the house which had later been the Genii Emmii's room. Here they had played, the guide said, and written most of the little books. Here the Twelves would feel at home if anywhere. Before they left Haworth, they prospected on foot the last stage of the Young Men's journey. Then they bicycled back, their plans laid in detail.

As they ran into the house, the drawing-room seemed to be full of people.

"Come in here a minute, children," called Mrs. Morley. They went in, wondering what was afoot. Their father was there, and another man they did not know: and Max's heart turned uncomfortably on seeing the reporter from the newspaper.

"Maxy," said his mother, "this is Mr. Kettlewell and he thinks he may have found one of your soldiers. Apparently there is a bit in the paper about it."

"Yes, we saw it," said Max slowly. But what he was seeing now, what his gaze was fixed upon, was Butter. Standing on the mantelpiece, martial and stately and wooden, surveying the drawing-room with a fixed though benign patriarchal stare. Max walked towards him and held up his hand as if to take him, and decided against it.

"Do you recognize him? Is he one of yours?" asked the farmer.

Recognize him! Recognize Butter Crashey, patriarch of the Twelves! Max smiled. But he supposed that to them he must look very wooden.

"Yes, I do. Thank you," he said. "Thank you very much."

And he and Jane and Philip all stood silently gazing at the patriarch and each thinking the same thing: what would happen, if Crashey, recognizing the Genii's voices, should hold up his tiny arms and then bow and smile, and speak to them?

"Mr. Kettlewell found him in a field on his farm, Max," said his father. "How did he get there? Where do you suppose the rest are?"

"I don't *exactly* know," Max said slowly, hedging.

"But it seems that people in the village are saying that you must know where they are. Our friend here, from the paper, has heard the professor's not coming and the soldiers are to be given to Haworth," Mr. Morley said.

"Have you put off that professor, Philip?" asked his mother.

"Yes, Mrs. Morley, I have," Philip said.

"What did you tell him then?" she went on. "That the soldiers were lost?"

This was a facer. The Genii Philippi looked helplessly at the chief Genii Maxii as if for guidance. The Genii Maxii stared back, his huge eyes larger than usual.

"I said they'd be going to Haworth," Philip admitted. "You see," he added quickly, clutching at a straw, "they will be, if they're ever found, won't they, it's obvious, it's what Max wants, and everyone wants——"

Wooden Soldiers Going to Haworth

"Yes, if it can be proved they belonged to the Brontës," Mrs. Morley said.

"Do you, or don't you, know where they are, Max?" his father said.

"Not at this exact minute," Max said again.

"Well, Max, are they safe?" his mother said. "They should be looked after, the sooner they are put into the museum's care the better. Is that what you've been doing this morning?" she finished.

"They're safe and they're going there," Max said, stubbornly. "We can't explain any more."

"I do hope they are safe," put in the reporter, "because everyone knows about this offer of £5,000, and everyone who read today's paper knows Mr. Kettlewell found one, and the whole world can come out here seeing if they can pick them up. I think you've made the right decision, young man, but I've never known anyone so difficult to get a story out of. What happened?" he almost shouted, rising to his feet. Had he but known it, this was at once enough to put Mr. Morley on his son's side. Good for Max, why should he tell? He slapped Max's behind and laughed. He could not help being glad Max was so hard to get a story out of, he was the same himself. Max half-smiled and bit his lips, as everyone laughed. Mr. Kettlewell leaned forward.

"I reckon this 'ere will make you laugh, me lad," he said. "When I'd found yon soldier" (and he pointed to B. Crashey), "I could have taken me oath, aye, on t' Bible if need be, that he were alive. I saw him move, I tell tha, and t' dog here did and all. Aye, and he had a lile cotton poke with him, full of hen-corn, and yon moved and all, as if he were pulling on it. Theere! See what your laiking and your soldiers can do at a sober man!" and he slapped his knee and threw back his head and laughed. "See what comes of all this daft goin-on about t' old Brontës!"

Max did not laugh at all, he looked very grave; until the Genii Philippi, almost too suddenly and loudly, but really very cleverly, let out a hoot and showed the other two what was needed.

But the reporter stared fixedly at Max.

"He's not laughing," he said. "And he won't tell."

"Everybody'll soon know," Max stated as if this were his last word. "And then you can put it in the paper."

"Bless the boy," said the exasperated newspaper man. "What's the good of that, when they *know*!"

Chapter 23

The Chief
Genius Brannii

By Monday afternoon a strange and delightful rumour was
spreading round the Morleys' village and the small town of
Haworth itself, and even villages further afield. It centred
upon Mr. Kettlewell's land, but its exciting possibilities seemed to
tinge the whole countryside with enchantment.

Two little girls had wandered off on Monday morning to a field
of oats quite near to their cottage, and sitting down upon the sunny
green edge between corn and wall had been rapt in some secret
game, when they had heard a rustle in the oats as if a field mouse
were coming through it. The stalks jostled. The little girls lay on
their stomachs and gazed into the silvery gold world of the oats,
imagining themselves inside it. And at a short distance from the
path they saw a column of little men threading their way through
this forest, holding a tiny blue flag aloft. They heard thin, cautious
singing. One little girl said later that at times she could recognize
the song and it was the nursery rhyme about the brave old Duke of
York. The troop of tiny men, dressed like soldiers, some with
feathers in their hats, seemed so at home in the oats, the sun was
so hot, and the green field-path was so silent and magic, that the
little girls only nudged each other, and exclaimed, and gasped, and
lay watching as if this were nothing more than you might expect
in a field of oats on an August day.

They watched the soldiers return from their exercise. They saw
three of the smallest of them swarm up stalks of swaying oats and
throw down the ripe grains to those waiting below. They saw them
sit in a stately ring in a small clearing and eat the grains. They even
saw one, braver than the rest, come out on to the green path ahead

of them and look each way, and gaze up to the heavens, holding on
his tall hat. They kept quite still, but he seemed to sense they were
there and marched quickly back on his stumpy legs. They heard a
distant whisking, crackling noise like talk and laughter.

Now when at last the little girls tore themselves away, the
soldiers having disappeared further into the oats, and ran home and
told what they had seen, their fathers said it was a pity they hadn't
clicked hold on t' wooden soldiers, for they'd heard t' tale Mr.
Kettlewell had been telling folks about t' one that *he'd* found, and
it fair capped all! Aye, and where there was one they reckoned it
were a rum 'un if there weren't more, somewhere gain-hand t' spot;
and if this lot were them that had belonged t' old Brontës, they
were fit to fetch five thousand pounds, or so folk said. And what
had gotten them now? Wheere were they, then? Gone off into t'
field, they said. Gone off? And hidden themselves in t' straw? Nay,
come, they knew it were to no use pretending that wooden soldiers
were wick, yon were nobbut a game, like.

But the children said they had both seen them, and heard the
singing; they were different heights, too, not all the same, and yes,
they had tall hats like the one Mr. Kettlewell found. They said all
this so seriously that it was difficult to disbelieve them.

Their fathers made excuses to take strolls along that field, and
even lay on their fronts (when they hoped no one was looking) and
gazed, feeling daft, into the oats. And they thought, once down,
how possible it all sounded, the world of the nodding grain was so
secret, and reminded them of their boyhood. People in neighbouring houses heard, people in the villages and from Haworth. Mr.
Kettlewell's fields had a good sprinkling of visitors over their
footpaths, some searching for their lost childhood, some thinking
of five thousand pounds.

Stumps had warned the Twelves and they went deep, deep into
that corn, and lay low; except for the midshipmen, who would
every now and then swarm up a silver stalk and peep out over the
whispering, pale gold sea.

It was talked of in shops and post offices and at the museum itself. It is strange how quickly a thing people would like to believe
runs round. This was a lovely thing, not only that the soldiers

belonging to their Brontës should be found by that little boy, a newcomer, but that they should also be alive! Did it not all fit in with the report of their disappearance? And where were they going to? What were they doing, in the corn?

At the museum, where the reporter spent some of the early afternoon, they said no, they had heard nothing about the Young Men coming to Haworth, or even being certainly found, they only hoped it was true. Though they themselves felt doubtful whether toys of wood could survive.

Bill brought the news to the Morleys, after lunch, when he had been home. He told Mr. Morley what was being said: and if it were right, hadn't their Max best go and seek his soldiers in Mr. Kettlewell's field? For he didn't see why some other body should collar the five thousand pounds, if yon were t' road things was going, nor let them get takken to America if he, Max, were agin it.

This was kind of Bill. And it was alarming to the Genii. The last thing they wanted was this rumour getting about until both Butter and the rest of the company were safely at Haworth. They could only hope that the Twelves would be careful, and that they would not get lost in the corn, and that they would be able to find them that night, and that all the people would have gone home to bed and not be hanging around.

But of course they said nothing of all this, and their guarded manner made Bill all the more certain there was some mystery, as he always had been: but what the mystery was he did not know. And why should it not, perhaps, be, that this rumour was true? Bill went home again and into the inn after tea believing it was true. And since he was known to work for Mr. Morley, the people in the inn thought he ought to know and began to believe it as well.

In the late afternoon that day Christopher Howson rang up Philip (as planned) and asked him, in very careful words, if he would like to come over and stay the night? And Philip reported, also in very careful words, that he had been asked by Christopher to go over there and stay the night. He did not say he was going, but his mother assumed it, and thus Philip avoided telling lies. It was very decent of Christopher to do this, as he hardly knew Philip, and he was dying to know where Philip was going that night, and Philip would not tell him. Philip bicycled off with a secret supply of supper in the direction of the Howsons' village, which lay north of Haworth.

Max took Beurre Crashey (as he was sometimes, in their Napoleonic moods, known by the Young Men) up to bed with him that night. When he was safely in and settled down, he lifted Butter from the window-sill and put him upon his pillow, where he sat cross-legged in a hollow of his own near Max's ear and they had a long and absorbing conversation. So close and comfortable was it that Butter did not have to shout nor Max to strain his ears. And Max asked many questions, about the Young Men, and their life in Angria, and heard about the Twelves' town, and about the great Glasstown, Verdopolis, which they built later. And he heard tales of Bravey's Inn, and Stumps's Island, and of battles and adventures and cannibals and heroes and heroines. He dared to ask too about their everyday life in the parsonage at Haworth, about the Genii Tallii, Emmii, and Annii. Last of all he asked about the Chief Genius Brannii, and Butter laughed with glee and at the same time with affection and said: "What a Genius he was! What a warm heart, bursting with love and admiration! Such artfulness and ingenuity, too, with which he endowed Sneaky! Such bravery and spirit, with which he made Stumps! Such haughty manners when he chose, like the Duke! Such comic mischief, like those midshipmen! Such bombast and boasting and exaggeration! Such tricks and spite, let it be confessed! Such a lift to the elbow, oh dear me, much like the hard-drinking Bravey. Emptying with the most perfect steadiness (I mean steadiness of supply and not steadiness of hand) glass after glass and bottle down his well-in-those-matters-tried-throat!"

And what about you, Butter, what did he give you? Max wanted to ask. There must have been something of him in you! You're so kind and dignified and calm and always able to arrange things, and you love the Twelves. And the chief thing about you, Butter, is that they all love you. And so do I. There must have been something in the Genius Brannii that was like you.

But he found it hard to say all this, so he contented himself with thinking it. And after a pause Butter broke out again:

"What a Genius! What invention! The things he imagined for us to do, and the way he told them. Alas," he finished after a minute's silence, "how are the mighty fallen! Few people now read the adventures that he wrote." And he brushed away a small, glistening tear.

Then they went on to talk of that night's march, and the plan of the Genii Philippi. Butter was well pleased at it, and rubbed his hands, and seeing Max was sleepy, and indeed slept, he lay down himself in his comfortable hollow and slept too.

And neither of them thought, until long afterwards, that this was perhaps the last occasion they would have for such a good conversation, friends as they were, and what a kind chance it was that had brought Butter Crashey back to the Genii Maxii for that night.

Jane woke Max and they were soon spinning down the hill with Butter Crashey in Max's bike basket. They did not approach Mr. Kettlewell's land by the lane and the gate (which led on down to the pack horse bridge) but kept to the main road and leaving their bikes turned off down another footpath to reach the cornfield. They did not want to pass the farmyard in case any persistent people, like that reporter, were still lurking near in the hopes of seeing the strange sight those little girls had seen.

But there was nobody about.

The next problem was how to find the Twelves, hidden in this dense forest of grain, restore their patriarch to them, and put them on the right road.

But as Max followed Jane along the path to the point where they had seen them enter the corn, he thought that this was probably no problem at all, now that they had Butter. "Revere this man Crashey," the chief Genii Brannii had said, "because secrets are intrusted to him which others cannot know."

"Will you be able to find them, and lead them out to the road, oh patriarch?" Max said, as Jane stopped.

"Undoubtedly," said he. Max put him down and he paused a minute on the edge of the oats looking both ways, taking a step here and a step there, and at last, like a questing creature, plunged off into the dark, whispering forest with a confident and determined step.

The Chief Genius Brannii

Max and Jane returned to where the footpath joined the road and waited. They talked low, in whispers, Max telling Jane some of the tales Butter had recounted in the pillow talk. They wondered how he would find them, setting off into that forest with every stalk like every other stalk. Jane looked up at the vanishing piece of moon and hoped it might stay clear to guide the Twelves. Max had the idea, then, of turning on his bike lamp and leaving it shining at the edge of the field. He went to fetch it from the road's edge and it was then he saw the motor-car.

Max's heart jumped.

Somebody got out of the motor-car and followed him back to Jane.

Max did not like this at all. Jane stood up.

The man shone a torch at them, and looked closely at Max.

"I think you can tell me where these wooden soldiers are, can't you?" he said, in an unpleasant tone of voice which tried to be friendly.

Max and Jane said nothing.

"You're the boy that found them, aren't you?" he said to Max, and his voice was rougher. Max could see no use in denying it. He nodded. He was too frightened to speak.

"Well, what are you hanging about here for at this time in the night? Where are they, eh? Hidden somewhere near here? Or is someone bringing them? I know there have been daft rumours about this field. But there's no smoke without fire."

Max thought that they must say something, simply to keep the man at bay. Jane came to the rescue.

"But what did you want them for?" she said innocently and softly.

"There's a man in America willing to give five thousand for them, they say. Come on, now. Where are they?"

He took hold of Max's shoulder and began to shake him. Jane saw another motor-car's lights in the distance climbing up the hill towards them. She waited, planning what she would do. It was not near enough yet, but it was the only chance.

"We don't exactly know," Max was saying in a voice quiet with fear.

"You must know. What're you lurking about here for else?" the man growled. Jane darted into the middle of the road, held up both her arms and waved them wildly, while she jumped in the air.

The motor-car stopped at once in a gentle way as if it must belong to a helpful person. So Jane thought. She ran to the door, her face wild with fright. She could hear Max suddenly screaming. (He was having his arm twisted.)

"Jane! Jane! What are you doing here?" said Mr. Rochester.

"Oh do come!" Jane sobbed. "Quickly!" Mr. Howson jumped out at once, but there was no longer any alarm. For the intruder had rushed for his own motor-car, was starting the engine, and roared off down the road not waiting for anything.

"What is it, what on earth are you children doing, out here at this hour?" Mr. Howson said. "Max! What's the matter?"

Jane clung to Mr. Rochester and Max took hold of his other arm. His face was shining with the tears which he could not help crying at the arm-twisting.

"It was a man. Trying to make us tell him where the soldiers were," Max explained in a choky voice.

"Well, where are they?" asked Mr. Howson, naturally enough.

Jane and Max looked at each other across Mr. Rochester's stomach (he ought to be wearing an ulster, Jane thought) and nodded in agreement.

"They're coming," Max said.

"Through the oats," said Jane.

"They're marching to Haworth," said Max.

"This is the last night," she added, "and I thought they were going to get caught!"

Mr. Howson did not know what to think. He stared at the Morleys in turn, and then at the cornfield and then at the moon. He had in fact been sitting with an old man of his parish, a friend of his, in an outlying cottage, who had been ill for weeks and to-night had died. This was why he was out on this road at after two in the morning. Death was so solemn anyway, and made the watcher think such strange and mysterious thoughts about the nature of things, that Mr. Howson was not unduly surprised at finding Jane and Max and hearing a tale which seemed impossible.

"Coming?" he said questioningly, as he squeezed both their arms.

Max stooped down, adjusting his lamp on the ground.

"Yes. Here they are," he whispered.

In the light of the lamp, the Young Men filed out, singly and silent, the middies, Gravey, Bravey with the flag, Cheeky, Stumps, Sneaky, Parry, Ross, the Duke. And the patriarch last. They halted.

"So this was it. All the time," Mr. Howson said. He knelt down, gently, and looked at them. They were not alarmed. They shuffled, and stood at ease. The patriarch lifted up his arms to Max, and smiled.

Max knelt down by Mr. Howson and picked Butter Crashey up.

"This is the reverend Genii, oh Patriarch," he said, and he handed Butter to Mr. Howson. Mr. Howson held B. Crashey up, and as he looked at him the moon sidled out again and showed the patriarch smiling and nodding.

The Chief Genius Brannii

"I have long wanted to make your acquaintance, Butter Crashey, patriarch and oracle of the Young Men," said Mr. Howson, who had been re-reading all the Genii Brannii's stories since Max found the soldiers. There was a bright little cheer from the line of Twelves, all gazing up at the reverend Genii.

"The Young Men welcome you; it was a reverend Genii who first brought us to Haworth," explained Beurre Crashey, nodding his head.

Mr. Howson thought, I cannot believe it, and yet here they are before my eyes. Such is the power of genius to make things alive. So do creative genii echo their Creator. He put Butter down again with the rest.

He wanted to ask which was Sneaky, and Gravey and Stumps; the Duke he could pick out at once by his height. But he decided that enough had been said and that he must interrupt their march no longer. Max shone his torch at the road.

"Here you must cross a wide main road, Butter Crashey, and there may be motor-cars on it." He looked both ways anxiously. At the moment there was nothing, and the lights of Mr. Howson's motor-car lit it up. "Can you hurry them across, perhaps?" he suggested.

The Duke had brought the men to the very verge, where they stood ready.

"Young Men, at the double!" ordered Crashey. And the whole column bowed their heads, bent their elbows, picked up their heels, and ran across the road like sprinters. Jane laughed with delight, as each passed in the beam of the headlights, she had never seen them all run before.

"Splendid," said the reverend Genii, as they followed. "Utterly splendid."

They were panting visibly as Max stopped to see them gather on the other side. The middies slapped their chests and gasped. Then they formed into their usual double column, and set off instinctively to join the footpath which led to Haworth and the parsonage museum.

Jane looked up at Mr. Howson and took his arm again.

"Will you come?" she pleaded. "In case . . . in case. . . ." What could go wrong now? They were nearly there. But there was the man in the motor-car, who might perhaps think of waiting at the museum. There might even be difficulties in Philip's plan.

"Jane, I will most certainly come," said Mr. Rochester eagerly, "if I am invited. I'm greatly honoured," he said seriously. And she knew he meant it. "Besides which," he went on, "I shan't sleep happy in my bed till you are all, Young Men and Morleys, safe in yours."

He brought his motor-car in to the side of the road and locked it. He and Jane followed Max, whose lamp they could see ahead acting as a pillar of fire (as Phil said) to the Twelves.

From her bicycle basket, Jane had fetched a large, oval, thong-covered thing which she now carried under her arm. Mr. Howson stared at it curiously. It was the Ashanti drum.

"You see, we thought they deserved a kind of triumphal entry," Jane explained. "As there are only three—no, four Genii, to see them. This is the drum they used in our attic."

The Genii watched over the last stage of the journey, Max holding back the gates in the walls for the Young Men to file through.

The others were near enough to hear their shrill cheer as they recognized their former home.

Chapter 24

The Twelves
Reach Home

Philip was stiff with keeping still, tired with keeping awake and miserable with waiting. He was also faintly, just faintly, uneasy. As he leaned against the wall, sitting on the hard floor, in the Brontës' nursery, which had later been the Genii Emmii's room, it was difficult not to feel that it was all rather ghostly. He had his bike lamp, but that sometimes made things worse, as he played it round the walls. And anyway he was afraid of someone seeing the light. He had camped himself behind the door so that he could hide, if someone did, perhaps, hearing a sound, come upstairs and open it.

For he could not keep absolutely still, it was more than flesh and blood could do. At first he had done so, lurking last in the little room, closing its door when he heard no more visitors' footsteps and then simply praying curators and others would assume it to be empty. He stood frozen by this door for quite half an hour. This was good discipline and he was rather proud of it.

After that, as the evening wore on, he ate his food, and prowled stealthily round, looking at things and peeping from the window. There was Emily gazing rather timidly, in a visionary way (as if she were looking out over the moors) in the copy of Branwell's painting. Here were drawings the four Genii had scratched on the walls. On show were some of their pencil drawings too. As the daylight finally died away over the wild stretch of moors which he could see from the window, Philip found it difficult not to feel that the four Genii were really rather uncomfortably close. And the whole thing would be nicer when it was over than it was now. It was a good thing that he was at last in the secret, to perform this part. He thought Max would have disliked it; and he was sure Jane would have refused point blank.

Then he must have slept, with his head on his knees, for he woke up cold and stiff. He looked at his watch. It was half-past three. He was delighted. Surely this vigil must be nearly over, and so far the plan had worked.

He crept over to the window, sat on the sill and peered out. There were bike lamps in the garden. They were here. Thank goodness. Then Philip's heart turned rather uncomfortably at seeing a tall, adult figure beside Jane. This was not part of the plan: who was this? Had the museum people woken up after all and seen them? He supposed there might be a fuss at his staying inside all night, but apart from that they were doing no harm, indeed they were conferring on Haworth a priceless gift (according to Seneca D. Brewer) and the fact that they had to do it this way must simply be accepted.

Philip undid the catch and very gently pushed up the window. Jane shone her lamp up to show she had seen him. Then he saw who was with her. Nobody said a word.

There was Max, shining his lamp upon the foot of the creeper along by the dining-room window. There was Janey with that ridiculous drum which was enough to wake all Haworth, let alone the museum people.

When the Duke, the patriarch, Sneaky, Parry and Ross, and all the rest realized how they could regain their home, they ran eagerly across the lawn from near Jane's feet, mountaineered up the grass bank and gathered near the creeper.

"The great moment is at hand," said the patriarch. "Who shall lead us?"

"Stumps," said several voices, remembering how Stumps had climbed up the other creeper.

"I suggest the Duke," said Ross, "the noblest first."

The Duke demurred and suggested Ross. Parry and Sneaky, also, after all, kings of the Ashanti, were jealous of this and Sneaky showed it by his sinister laugh.

"Not I," said Cheeky, "lest any man slip, fall, and need to be made alive."

"That is an encouragement, before our dangerous climb," said Gravey in a mournful tone. The middies laughed.

"Come along, come along, eat, drink and be merry!" called Bravey, dancing a fandango on the top of the bank and nearly rolling down it. "Show your mettle, men."

Oh goodness me, thought Max, if only they would not argue now.

"Let the middies go, let the young rascals climb the rigging,"

said Stumps, who had, in the very beginning, been one of them, "and I will follow them."

Jane, like Max, was tired of waiting. She was afraid their lights and commotion would wake someone. She put the drum down on the ground, knelt by it and began to beat, very softly, a rapid tattoo.

This was enough for Monkey. He let out a shrill cry: "Up the rigging and down the plank!" dived into the rustling creeper and led the way. He was followed quickly by Crackey and Tracky jostling for place, and Stumps, the hero of so many escapes and adventures, went after them. Max could not help starting forward to whisper to Stumps. "Au revoir," said Stumps smiling, and he began to sing, in his eager light voice:

> *"Marlbrook s'en va-t-en guerre,*
> *Marlbrook s'en va-t-en guerre,*
> *Marlbrook s'en va-t-en guerre,*
> *Il ne sait quand reviendra."*

The rest took up the air as they climbed and crawled and swung and panted, moving first up and then along towards the open window and the light of Philip's torch. But as some knew the English words better than the French version, and sang lustily, and very suitably:

> *"We won't go home till morning,*
> *We won't go home till morning,*
> *We won't go home till morning,*
> *And a-hunting we will go,"*

the sound Philip heard, leaning out, was as confused, merry and spirited as sparrows in the eaves.

Max and Jane knelt by the creeper, watching each Young Man in turn start his climb. Jane picked up Gravey, removed his coil of string and wished him good-bye. Gravey smiled before he set off. Mr. Howson, dumb with surprise and delight, stood gazing into a gap in the leaves to see them pass and trying to make out the song. Mr. Howson had not had long to get used to their voices.

As the patriarch, last by right, prepared to follow the rest, he turned to Max, held up his arms in the familiar gesture, smiled and bowed.

"Good-bye, oh Butter Crashey," Max said, very subdued. "I shall come and visit you."

"Good-bye, Genii Maxii," said the patriarch. "You will always find me at home."

Then he turned about, plunged gladly into the creeper and started to climb. Max sniffed.

They could hear when Butter's slow and stately climb was over, for a reverential cheer went up from the window-sill. Jane stopped beating her drum. The Genii Philippi had helped those who needed help, grasping them gently as their heads appeared and lifting them to safety. As Butter arrived, he put him with the rest, drew in his head and quietly closed the window, fastening the catch. Grey curtains of light in the sky promised the dawn.

"Welcome home, Young Men, the place awaits you," Philip said formally, stooping to peer at them, arrayed on the sill.

The Twelves were surveying the nursery with shrill cries of delight. It was clear that they recognized it and were pleased to be there.

Philip tiptoed down the stairs and let himself out of the front door.

And so, their last journey over, the Twelve adventurers returned to their ancestral home.

Chapter 25

Night Life

In the morning the troop of wooden soldiers, twelve in number, and of a design like that described by Branwell Brontë in *The History of the Young Men*, were found upon the window-sill of the nursery at the museum. Beside them was stuck a little blue paper flag, from a recent flag day.

They stood in proud, martial order, two by two in their usual manner: Crackey and Tracky, Monkey and Cheeky, Bravey and Gravey, Sneaky and Stumps, Parry and Ross, the Duke of Wellington and the patriarch Crashey. But the visitor who found them, seizing one with an exclamation, did not know which it was he seized, nor what were the names of the rest. How are the mighty fallen!

Everybody in authority came to see, as well as the early visitors. The window was closed, bolted and undamaged. The house wall and creeper showed no signs of having been climbed. How had they got here?

Why, somebody had brought them yesterday, no doubt, and left them just before closing time, and here they were. It was odd that whoever it was who had found them had said nothing about it. But perhaps they had thought it best to keep quiet because of the offer of five thousand pounds from the American professor. And perhaps this small boy from the farm in the neighbouring hamlet knew all about it.

They rang up the Morleys to ask if this set of soldiers, which had appeared overnight in the museum, were the ones Max had found in their attic, and which had mysteriously vanished. Yes, answered

Mr. Morley, these were the ones and his son was glad they had reached the museum, which was certainly their home.

Now this was all very well, and they thanked Max kindly, but was he sure of the identity of the Twelves? Were these indeed the soldiers beloved by the Brontës, written about by Branwell and Charlotte, the originators of so many games and so many stories? And if he was sure, how was he sure?

They rang up the newspaper, to report the arrival of the twelve soldiers at Haworth, in a mysterious way, overnight. For all the newspaper had printed that morning was a small paragraph, not very high up, describing a delightful rumour which had flown round the Brontë neighbourhood after two small girls were said to have seen a troop of live little soldiers in a cornfield. The newspaper did not deny the truth of this, it simply described it, and the reporter had mentioned again what Mr. Kettlewell found and thought he saw, and the odd behaviour of the young boy who first found the soldiers. And now these same soldiers had reached their destination, in mysterious circumstances. People could think what they liked about it, following on the delightful rumour. What if, the reporter asked next day, the little men had marched back home? (Perhaps this is what he wanted to think himself.)

Meanwhile, visitors flocked in even greater numbers than usual to the museum, to see the Twelves, the Young Men, now standing grouped round their tiny magazines. A few, who had read the stories, would say, Oh *that* must be the Duke! And this must be Butter Crashey, the patriarch, one hundred and forty! But most, who had not, looked at them with curiosity and pleasure, in case they were the beloved of the young Brontës, but nevertheless thought they looked very like any other wooden soldiers, and asked again how could anyone be sure?

For how had they been saved from destruction and collected together, in the first place, when Branwell reported all but a few as perished? To this there seemed no answer. And how had they reached the attic at the Morleys' farm? Again, nobody knew, and one theory was as good as another; and Max could not help, for upon this part in their varied history the Young Men had remained resolutely dumb. (But this was no more than Branwell had always said they did when questioned sometimes on their past. It was evidently in their make-up, as it was in Max's, and Mr. Morley's, to be sometimes wooden.) And neither could Mr. and Mrs. Morley help, upon these pressing points. All they knew was that the Twelves had been found in their attic, played with by their son, and had disappeared from their house after the professor wrote to the newspaper. They admitted there was some mystery as to how the soldiers had reached the Parsonage Museum. Three nights running, Mrs. Morley, who was a light sleeper, had thought she heard movements, had thought her children were up to some nocturnal caper, and had noticed both their yawns in the daytime, and the absence of food from her larder. And Mr. Morley knew that Max and Jane and Phil were not telling all they knew, but he was not going to press them. And Mrs. Morley kept to herself (and Max) the strange noises she had once heard in the attic, and the movement seen out of the corner of her eye; because both the sound and the movement had stopped so suddenly that she thought she must have been mistaken. But now, she wondered: what with the farmer, and the little girls, and Max himself. And when Max said it was true, she could only be sad that she had not seen more of it.

So, by and large, the Morleys were no help.

Then the experts and the authorities got into touch with that nearby brontyfan, the Reverend Mr. Howson, who seemed well versed in Branwell's stories, and who was himself a member of the Brontë Society and wrote papers about them and addressed meetings and one thing and another.

And Mr. Howson visited the museum with the young Morleys, after hours, when they could have the Young Men to themselves in the nursery. Mr. Howson came out of that delightful encounter absolutely convinced, from his conversation with Butter, that these were the Twelves (which he, of course, had never doubted) and moreover, that the Duke was the Duke; and which was Stumps, and which the Kings, Sneaky and Parry and Ross; and which poor Gravey, and cheerful Bravey, and Cheeky the surgeon, and Monkey and Crackey and Tracky. He was able, indeed, to tell the authorities which was which, and although he had better means of knowing, he could point to Crackey's crack and Stumps's stumpy legs and Gravey's sardonic face, which was all other people could understand. And this he did, and because he was so sure, and he was a grown-up and a parson and a brontyfan, his word was taken. No one doubted any more that these were the Young Men. As to Seneca D. Brewer, who flew over to see them, he saw no reason to doubt anything, he would much rather believe. He took colour photographs of them, arranged round their magazines, and gave the Morleys five pounds each, and invited Phil to America.

But what about Butter Crashey and the noble Twelves? Were they doomed to perpetual frozendom, now that they were on show in their ancestral mansion? What a dull and gloomy life for such characters, well might Gravey moan and Stumps kick over the traces. No; they kept their faculties as sharp as ever, and indulged in night life. What they got up to at nights was nobody's business, and only occasionally were they unable to get back again to where they were supposed to be, such was the boldness of Cheeky and Stumps, and the ingenuity of Sneaky. (Once, however, they were

Night Life

found in the kitchen, and it was thought to be somebody's joke.)

But in the daytime they rarely, rarely show themselves for what they are. Very occasionally, some child or child-hearted person catches sight of Butter Crashey with his arms upheld (Max never knew if this was to make himself taller, or if it was simply to say, Lift me up); or Bravey with his elbow raised as if to drink; or Monkey executing a few steps of an incredibly quick reel; or the Duke yawning; or Stumps singing, or Sneaky striking some attitude, or Gravey groaning. When they fetch others to see, ten to one they are unlucky, and the Twelves simply stare from blurred wooden faces all looking very much alike.

But when Max goes and is lucky enough to find the room empty and picks up B. Crashey, and says gently: "It is the Genii Maxii"; then Butter wriggles, warm and taut as a lizard in Max's fingers, and Max sees their blurred wooden faces change delightfully into bright living ones, each different, and all eager.

Afterword

Katherine Paterson

There is a certain kind of fantasy that the British seem to do better than we Americans. In a country where a hundred-year-old house seems practically new, and every respectable house has its own familiar ghost, it's easier to believe that twelve wooden soldiers could come alive after more than a century to seek adventures and find their way home again.

The Return of the Twelves was originally published in England with the title *The Twelve and the Genii* in 1962. The following year it won the British Library Association's Carnegie Medal, which is the equivalent of our Newbery Medal. I was a grown woman by then, so I never had a chance to read the book as a child. But it doesn't seem to matter. Butter Crashey and Stumps and the Duke are just as real to me now as they would have been forty years or so ago. It makes perfectly good sense to me that somehow the Brontës' toy soldiers should have ended up a hundred and twenty-five years later in the attic of a neighboring farmhouse under a loose board to be found by a curious eight-year-old and brought to life by the beat of an Ashanti drum.

I suppose some super realists among us would dismiss this tale as the old "toys brought to life story" or even as just another of those "little people tales." In a sense, *The Twelves* is both. Most children do bring their toys to life, though they may not, with lives crammed with afterschool enrichment activities and TV, have time to involve them in elaborate adventures in Africa or write books and magazines for them the way the young Brontës did. And who of us is not fascinated with tiny things?

182

Afterword

Doesn't the thought of small, living people thrill us all? I remember reading *Mistress Masham's Repose* when I was young. In that book some of the Lilliputians brought to England by Gulliver are discovered by a lonely orphan named Maria. I adored that book. I still do, as a matter of fact.

Max, in this book, has something (besides a loving family) that Maria lacks. He has, from the very beginning, an enormous respect for the little people. He never plays with them; he simply observes them, occasionally assists them, but tries always to do so without injuring their dignity.

It seemed quite fitting to me that Pauline Clarke uses the imagery of the story of Exodus as she describes the journey of the Twelves to their old home at the Haworth parsonage. Jane's feast is like manna in the wilderness and Phil's bicycle light is like the pillar of fire showing the way to the Promised Land.

But above all it is eight-year-old Max who loves the Young Men as the God of Israel loved his people. He knows each of them by name and character. He is saddened by their squabbling but patient with their imperfect natures. Although with one swoop of his giant hand he could save them and himself all kinds of trouble, he holds back. They must be allowed freedom to find their own way, even when it means making mistakes and running risks.

Yet, as much as I admire Max, I long to ask Pauline Clarke why he is quite so godlike. It is not that I find him unbelievable. I have known eight-year-old boys with just his solemn sense of responsibility who would have kept the secret of the Young Men from greedy adults and who would have respected the free will of their small charges. Yet the very qualities that make Max so admirable do keep the plot in rather neat bounds. Maria in *Mistress Masham's Repose* is not nearly so good or wise as Max, which tends to make her story scarier and funnier than his.

Still, it's not fair to criticize Max for not being Maria, any more than it would be fair to criticize Gravey for not being Stumps. People are different, which is one of the premises of this very enjoyable novel.

Each of us as readers has a right to choose what we will learn from reading a book. And because we are different people, we will hear different messages. *The Return of the Twelves* sent me back to the Bible, not just to Exodus, as I mentioned earlier, but to Genesis, where we read: "So God created man in his own image, in the image of God created he him; male and female created he them." The four Brontë children had breathed life into the Young Men, giving them facets of their own personalities, creating them in their own images. Later Max would bring the wooden men back to life, his imagination providing them with new adventures. It is no accident that the children of both families are called genii ('jē nē ī). Genii is the old plural of genius, a word with at least two meanings. The first refers to a person with exceptional creative and imaginative capabilities, the second to a guardian spirit. The original Brontës and the Morleys after them were genii in both senses.

It is in imagining that we echo what God did in creation. Wonderful books of fantasy like *The Return of the Twelves* not only remind us of that truth, but they help nourish our own imaginative powers. We may all be genii if we choose.